# THE HORRORS
## Terrifying Tales

### Book Two

# THE HORRORS
## Terrifying Tales

Book Two

*Edited by Peter Carver*

Red Deer
PRESS

PUBLISHED BY
Red Deer Press
A Fitzhenry & Whiteside Company
1512, 1800–4 Street S.W.
Calgary, Alberta, Canada T2S 2S5
www.reddeerpress.com

CREDITS
Edited for the Press by Peter Carver
Copyedited by Kirstin Morrell
Text design by Erin Woodward
Cover illustration by Peter Ledwon
Printed and bound in Canada by Friesens for Red Deer Press

ACKNOWLEDGMENTS
Financial support provided by the Canada Council, and the Government of Canada through the Book Publishing Industry Development Program (BPIDP).

THE CANADA COUNCIL | LE CONSEIL DES ARTS
FOR THE ARTS | DU CANADA
SINCE 1957 | DEPUIS 1957

NATIONAL LIBRARY OF CANADA CATALOGUING IN PUBLICATION
Carver, Peter, 1936–
The horrors : terrifying tales / Peter Carver.
ISBN 0-88995-313-9 (v. 1).--ISBN 0-88995-338-4 (v. 2)
1. Horror tales, Canadian (English)  I. Title.
PS8605.A775H67 2005      jC813'.6     C2005-902477-1

# Contents

# Introduction

There's a memory I have of sitting around a fire and someone telling the story with the punchline: "Johnny, give me your liver. . . ." And another of reading a tale of the wendigo, the elusive spirit of the northern wilderness that lures its victims deeper, ever deeper into the dark woods at night.

Creepy tales, both. The kind that make you shiver a little and peer beyond the circle of lamplight on a blustery night.

We've got some stories like that for you here. The second volume of *The Horrors* consists of stories that have been written specially for this collection, stories about ghosts and vampires and werewolves, and a prince who likes to experiment with dead bodies. But also stories about the scary events and characters that can appear in the most ordinary of lives. A drama teacher who is not at all what she seems. A babysitter preyed on by a too-active imagination. A cruise ship where ghastly plots abound. The madness that comes when you're trapped in a snowstorm.

And then there's the teen-aged healer who discovers the heart of evil that beats within the body of someone close to her.

The stories in *The Horrors: Book Two* come from the keyboards of some of our leading authors for teens—and also from several emerging writers who share their darker imaginings with you. When we put out a call for contributions to our original horror story collection, we received so much that was wonderfully macabre that we realized we had sufficient material for two volumes, rather than just the one we had planned for. The first came out in the spring of 2005; now this.

So here you are, a feast of fiction to lose yourself in, to keep you awake on those long, quiet, solitary nights. Settle in—and enjoy.

*Peter Carver*
*Everton, January 2006*

# THE DRUMMER

## Louise Wadsworth

Alice appeared in the doorway, out of bed long after bedtime.

"Nolan," she said, "I can hear the Drummer coming."

I turned down the TV.

"What drummer is that then?"

"*The* Drummer," she said.

She was holding a rag doll with hair like her own, twisting the long, blond tresses through her fingers.

"Aren't you hurting your dolly like that, Alice?" I asked. "Poor dolly. Take her back to bed now, love."

"I can't, Nolan."

"Why not?"

"She's afraid."

I knew then it must have been a nightmare. I used to have nightmares when I was a child. They woke me up screaming and then I forgot them. But Alice looked like she hadn't forgotten, and was I not the babysitter after all?

"Come here then, love. Come and watch TV with me for a bit, and bring dolly too. What's her name?"

"Lucy."

"Okay then, Lucy and Alice. Come and sit here by the fire. There's a funny show about to begin. We'll all three of us sit and watch it."

She sat down by the crackling fire and stared at the screen. The flames chattered and danced. I put on another log and felt my eyes grow heavy with comfort.

"Are you warm enough, Alice?"

"Yes, thank you, Nolan."

"Would you like some water?"

"No, thank you, Nolan."

She had nice little manners, this little Alice, but the TV program was too old for her, and when the commercials came on I turned them off.

"To bed now, Alice."

"But I can still hear him, Nolan,"

"Hear who?"

"The Drummer."

I listened. There was nothing.

"I don't hear any drumming, Alice," I said. "It's just the memory of a dream on you, that's all."

"But Nolan, it's getting louder all the time."

I looked at her sitting by me, with her dark, serious eyes and her dolly tucked under her chin.

"Listen again, Nolan," she begged me. "Listen."

I looked at my watch. It was nearly ten o'clock and she should be asleep. I was no kind of babysitter to let this continue.

"Now, Alice," I said, getting to my feet. "I'm listening as hard as I can and I hear nothing. You'll have to just believe me when I tell you it was a dream, that's all."

"But I can't go to sleep," said Alice, "until that Drummer stops."

She remained where she was, huddled on the ground with stubborn Lucy, both of them watching me like cats with their wide, waiting eyes. So this was real babysitting.

"Well then," I said.

I did not have any experience at real babysitting.

"Your mummy and daddy won't like this, they won't."

Silence.

"You don't want me to get into trouble now, do you, Alice?"

Silence again.

"Well, do you?"

"No, Nolan, but . . . " she trailed off, her voice small.

"But what?"

"What if he comes in my room?"

I sighed.

"He won't come in your room, Alice, because he doesn't exist."

But it was useless. I saw her fingers tighten deeper in Lucy's hair and her toes curl into the carpet. She was digging herself in, preparing to wait me out until her parents came home. I would look a very poor babysitter. I realized I would have to follow this child's own rules to win my way.

"What can I do then," I asked, "so you'll go back to bed?"

"You can find that Drummer, Nolan, and make him go away."

Well, that should be a simple thing, I thought. He can't be any-where to find. We'll look everywhere and then I'll send her to bed.

"All right, Alice," I said. "Come with me."

She hesitated, but then reached out her hand. I took it in my own and helped her up. I had only ever held a baby sparrow as fragile, fluttering inside my fingers with a tiny beat. I felt I would protect this child and keep her warm.

"Where shall we look first then, Alice?" I asked with great tolerance. "Behind the sofa?"

I saw by her face that she doubted my skill.

"Nothing's ever behind the sofa," she chastised me with a frown.

"Is it not?" I smiled. "Where then?"

She hesitated, as though unsure where to send me now I was hers to command. She turned Lucy's head and made her listen intently.

"He is not in the house," she said, after a moment, "but I can still hear the drum, so he's somewhere."

"Somewhere?" I asked, suspecting that now she had my cooperation she feared she would soon be proved wrong.

"Somewhere near," was all she could add.

"We will look once and once only," I warned.

We went first to the hall, cold away from the warming fire, cold with blue walls and tapping feet on bare tile. There was a draft coming in from a crack under the front door, and the small window was frosty.

"Jack Frost," I said, thinking she might smile at a children's tale. "But no one else."

"He's on the garden path," said Alice, "behind the house."

They have a long, wild garden, the Paynes, with branches and roses and a path that runs down to the river. There had been a path like that in my own childhood, a path I had thought led to another world until I grew too large and I could see its ending. But Alice was still little and the shadows on that path still spoke mysteries to her. I shivered suddenly at the memory of being small and in the dark and hearing . . . something.

"There are dark places on that path," said Alice. Her voice startled me back to her. "He is hiding there."

"No, he isn't," I replied. "No one is hiding anywhere."

But nevertheless I would have to go down that path and show her, and my coat was only light, being the kind of coat I wear when I am being picked up and dropped off in cars. She caught my thought.

"Wear daddy's coat," she said.

It was thick and warm and hanging on a peg in the hall. I took it.

"You are a great deal of a nuisance, Alice," I said, "and you'll be very lucky if I ever babysit you again."

But all the same I was smiling at her frowning, worried face.

We went down the hall to the big kitchen at the back. There was a huge mirror hung over the table and I laughed at myself drowned out in Mr. Payne's coat and at my two yellow-haired followers. They almost bumped into me as I stopped to open the door.

"Wait here," I told them, and stepped out.

The night air bit, though it was only October. I stood as still as the world about. How quiet it was! There was a moon to set the shadows alive; it made the frost sparkle; but not a whisper of anything. Even the river was mute.

"See?" I said. My voice almost broke the air. "All asleep."

But I knew she would take nothing less than my journey down the path and back again as proof that no one else was to be met upon it. So I strode out like a soldier and began.

"See, Alice?" I called. "Nothing at all!"

More steps I took. I was halfway down the garden when I stopped again. The frost on the path was glittering eyes. The grass was frozen. I turned and saw Alice framed in the doorway, herself a statue in the icy night with only her golden hair to warm her.

"Still nothing," I said, but then a quick sound—*Tum*—and gone again.

The sound had woken the air. I listened, and the grass listened, and the leaves on the ground listened. Something had changed, somewhere out on the path. A feeling of unease crept over me.

Is that a stirring of the wind in the branches, I thought? Is that a sigh of the winter sleep to come?

*Ra ta tum.*

I spun about. The path was empty, but a memory was trying to awaken in me, chilling my blood as cold as the frost.

Wait a minute, I thought. It's kids, fooling about. Someone's got an old snare drum and a stick to beat it.

*Tum, ra ta tum.*

They're playing down by the water, not meaning any harm.

*Tum ra ta tum.*

"Who's there?" I called. "What are you doing?"

*Tum ra ta tum!*

It was louder now. It was coming on the path. The path held mysteries again. The path held monsters.

"Nolan . . ." whispered Alice.

But I still couldn't see them. I should have been able to; the moon was bright. I stared till my eyes watered with cold. I stared as though my fear had frozen me to the ground.

"Nolan!" cried Alice. "Come back!"

The drum was faster, panting towards me. All the sensible thoughts in my head were eaten up by the empty path. There was only the drumbeat: no drummer.

*Tum ra ta tum!*

"Where are you?" I called.

*Tum ra ta tum ra ta tum ra ta tum!*

"Stop!"

"Run, Nolan!" screamed Alice.

I did, I did run. I ran so fast I stumbled almost to the ground, but the light from the doorway reeled me in. I swept Alice along in front of me and kicked the door shut behind us, slamming home the bolt. We stood wide-eyed and listening. For a moment there was quiet. Then:

*Tum ra ta tum ra ta tum ra ta tum!*

It was beating on the door!

"Come, Alice!" I cried.

I ran to the phone in the hall and dialed.

"Emergency services," said the woman's voice.

"Police!"

A moment.

"This is the police."

"This is number three, Willow Road, in. . . ."

*Tum ra ta tum ra ta tum ra ta tum!*

"He's coming in, Nolan!"

"In Mederway! Someone's trying to break into the house!"

*Tum ra ta tum!*

There was a loud bang. Alice screamed.

"They're coming in!" I cried. "Hurry!"

But I couldn't hear the voice at the other end. The drum was everywhere. I dropped the phone. I had to save Alice.

"Where do you hide?" I asked.

"In the closet, in my room."

I picked her up. She was light and trembling. The beat of the drum almost swallowed her up. It was louder and louder, coming through the kitchen. I hurtled up the stairs with her in my arms, my feet beating out their own rhythm on the tread. But the other rhythm was stronger. Alice cried out and dropped Lucy on the landing.

"Ssh!" I commanded.

Her bedroom door was open; it was all pink inside; pink walls, pink windows, pink ruffles. There was a big, white closet. She was crying out and beating her fists on my shoulders and face. The drum was a hammer inside me, trying to knock me over, but I pulled open the closet door and thrust her inside.

"Ssh!" I said, but she was really screaming now. I should have closed the bedroom door! I should have brought a knife! I didn't dare turn around. I piled into the closet after her and pulled the door tight. There was a blanket and I threw it over her, trying to hide her little bird heart.

"Ssh!"

But she couldn't have heard me. The drumming was everywhere. The room shook and the floor vibrated and the beat coursed through my head and my heart and my fingers. It captured my pulse and breathed itself into me, made me one with it. Faster and faster. Louder and louder. Deeper and deeper. We were one: me and the drum.

Pound, pound, pound!

Beat, beat, beat!

*Tum ra ta tum ra ta tum!*

Quiet.

I don't know how long I waited. Outside the closet, the world had come to an end. Inside, there was nothing but my breathing. I waited longer, straining for any sound, not daring to believe we had escaped. Still there was nothing.

The police will arrive any minute, I thought.

I couldn't be found hiding in a closet. I should meet them, try to explain. I pressed a gentle hand on the blanket.

"Stay very, very quiet, Alice," I whispered.

She obeyed.

I pushed the closet door open a crack. It was just the pink room, nothing more. I pushed it open wider and crept out. I felt dizzy with fear. Any moment, I thought, someone will leap out at me. They didn't. I shut Alice safely inside the closet and walked out of the bedroom.

On the landing Lucy lay face up with her eyes staring. I picked her up and took her with me down the stairs. I could hear the crackle of the fire from the sitting room; I could hear the tick of the clock from the hall. Whoever had broken into the house was gone now.

"But Mummy," said a voice, deep from my memory, "there's drumming outside the house."

I stopped dead in the hall. What was that? What?

"What, Nolan?" They both rolled over from their sleep. "What is it?"

"Wee Willie Winkie."

"You're dreaming, Nolan. Go back to sleep."

*Go back to sleep.* But I'd been too afraid, so I'd crept in between them and closed my eyes, and the drumming had gone away. In the morning all was forgotten. *He* was forgotten. The Drummer.

That was the memory that had beckoned to me on the path. That was the monster. I had heard his drum a long time ago, and now Alice too. Did only little children hear him?

No! I was grown, wasn't I? What I heard was real! What I heard could be caught, and questioned by the police, and charged with trespass!

So I hurried into the kitchen where the huge mirror hung and caught a glimpse of something drowned out in Mr. Payne's coat, with a thin, frosty face and dark, glittering eyes, and a small smile on its lips as it rested its chin on top of Lucy's blond locks. And when I started screaming it went away.

And that was how the police found me. Screaming.

I've had some time now, to think about what happened. It's still all mixed together, but sometimes a piece falls out and lets me look at it before being swept away again. Sometimes it's a piece of the fire or the TV program, and I don't mind those. But sometimes it's a piece of his face—an eye looking back at me or a mouth smiling. When that happens they have to increase my medicine. I never see Alice, or hear the drum.

They don't know whether it was the first or the fifth or the tenth blow that killed her. I used to stare down at my hands and wonder how. Then I realized it was as much her fault as mine, and I finally understood the secret of the Drummer.

Because when I was little and I heard him, my parents were cruel. They ignored me and knew it was nonsense. But when Alice heard him, I was the babysitter. I was paid to watch over her, to listen. When she told me she heard the drum, that was the first step on the path. When I went to look for the Drummer, that was the second. Alice made him real, but only because I let her.

I was saved back then, because no one believed me.

But he got me in the end, he did.

He got me.

*Turrrrrrum!*

## X X X X X

*Louise Wadsworth was born and raised in the shadow of England's Yorkshire Moors, home to ghosts, goblins, and extraterrestrials—a perfect place to acquire a healthy respect for the supernatural. She decided to travel using her secretarial qualifications to get work. Her first place to visit was Canada, which she liked so much she became a citizen. Louise is currently back in Europe, traveling to as many places as possible. This is her second published story, and she has a growing bottom drawer of unpublished tales that she hopes one day to terrify people with. "The Drummer" is based on a real event. She would like to hear from anyone who's heard the drumbeat too.*

# THE FIRST ASSIGNMENT: FEAR

## Anne Laurel Carter

*This diary was found under a sofa cushion at a Goodwill store. The store clerk distinctly remembered the mom who'd brought it in. She obviously didn't know a diary had been hidden in her sofa. They tried to contact her but she'd left town. Her daughter had disappeared a year earlier. "I'd just bought us a house," the mom said. "I did everything for her and the police suspect she ran away with a best friend to live on the streets. She'd mentioned it to her drama teacher. I haven't heard a word from her. She broke my heart. Kids."*

*Tuesday, September 6th, 2005, 4 p.m.*

I'm writing this locked in my front-hall bathroom. Today was my first day as a latchkey kid. Now that I'm in high school Mom's gone back to work so we can afford a house, not an apartment. (Thanks Mom—you better not be reading this!)

Coming in, I saw the door to the basement was ajar. I sensed someone on the other side, down there, waiting for me. I swear I heard the stairs—creaking. I grabbed the portable phone off the hall table and called Morgan right away—she'll be over in ten minutes. That's why I'm waiting in here with the door locked (safe) and writing in my journal. I can't tell Mom. She'll worry, and as she says, we're both supposed to be "on a new page."

Today was my first day at Toronto School of the Arts. Jason McPherson and I are the only kids from Laurier Middle School. Jason stuck to me all day. If he doesn't unstick I'll call him LePage.

It's weird trying to figure people out. There's two new kids I want to know better. Michelle wears pink mascara around her black eyes and has a nose ring. Very exotic. Rita has tattoos of fantasy characters all over her back and down both arms. She believes in other realities.

Miss Beatty didn't show up for drama class. The principal did. He said we'd be getting a supply until Miss Beatty gets back. Bummer. How could the head of the theater department not show up first day? The principal said she spent Labour Day weekend up north at her cottage and hadn't returned. "Her brother informed us she was exhausted after a season at Stratford," he said. "He thinks she booked off a few extra days."

I guess that's show biz. Or an ego. I waited all summer for Miss Beatty. She was at my audition to TSA last spring. She was pretty cool: black leather and high heels. Her lips were deep red and she spoke with a faint British accent as if she'd grown up on Shakespeare. Not that she said much. She had this air of superiority, like she was forcing herself to tolerate our company, yet she watched my every move. I'd blocked my audition scene carefully, moving back and forth between two chairs to show the anxiety of my character. Miss Beatty bowed her head when I finished. As if I were hopeless? I was sure I'd failed and would be joining Morgan at North Toronto Collegiate.

Acting is my dream. I didn't sleep that week, waiting for the results. I kept seeing Miss Beatty's long black hair—streaked dark red to match her lips—slink forward to hide her smile. When I got the news I was in, that's when I decided: it's weird trying to figure people out.

In June I met Miss Beatty outside the guidance office when I went to pick courses. I was tongue-tied and nearly asked for her autograph. Oh duh! Thank God I only asked what she thought of my audition. She laughed—not mean-spirited at all.

"You were good," she said. "Or you wouldn't be here. You'll be in my class. In September you'll do that role but stay put in one chair. You'll learn to show your fear through your voice and face and body. You'll imagine the thing you're most afraid of."

We'd just moved into this house. I'm still nervous whenever Mom's out.

"Like being alone and thinking someone's in the basement?" I asked her.

There's the doorbell. Morgan's here.

*Friday, September 9th, 4 p.m.*

The front door was unlocked when I got home. I was last out this morning and sure I locked it. I stood in the front hall listening for noises, debating what to do. This house means a lot to Mom. I opened the door to the basement . . . quiet. I decided to call Morgan and wait for her in the kitchen. Graduation from the bathroom!

Yesterday I asked Mom if we might have mice in the basement. She said yes. She's going to buy traps. (Oh, thanks, Mom—as if mousetraps are going to stop the freak in the basement).

First week at TSA is over. Miss Beatty is still absent. Today the principal introduced *Mr.* Beatty. Some kids groaned. He's filling in for his sister until she returns.

It's uncanny how much he looks like his sister except he has an expressionless, blank face. I hate his brush cut. And he walks stiffly, as if he's in pain, like he has shingles or something. He started class by unfolding a portable director's chair, then sat on its edge to look us over.

He said he was sorry about Miss Beatty. It was weird to hear him talk about his sister as if she wasn't coming back. "I hope to achieve great things with you this term, more than my sister could have imagined."

He told us to sit in a big circle. A boy with dark skin and short black hair that falls in a curtain over his eyes said, "I came to this school because of Miss Beatty. I'm not staying if she doesn't come back."

Mr. Beatty lowered his head. It was that same head-drop movement Miss Beatty had at my audition, only of course, no long hair. He glanced at the seating plan in his hands before he looked up again and said, "You're Osama, right?"

After 9/11, I wondered how anyone could live in North America with that name.

"I understand your wanting my sister for drama, but give me a chance. What's your worst fear, Osama?"

Osama laughed nervously. "I don't know."

"Think about it."

The class was so quiet I could hear Jason wheezing beside me.

"You mean like falling off a boat and being attacked by hungry sharks? Or being hated and tortured?"

Mr. Beatty's voice went very quiet. "Which one is it, Osama?"

"What makes you think I'd tell you?"

"As the Great One, Miss Erika Beatty, used to say, theater is about human emotion. You need to explore yours if you want to stay in this class. Fear is the strongest human emotion we have. Stronger than love. Sharing your worst fear will start your adrenaline pumping."

Out of nowhere, Rita said, "Is she dead? Your sister?"

Mr. Beatty's mouth formed a soundless O. "What a horrible question."

We all stared at Rita. "Sorry. It was the way you said it . . . I wondered, that's all."

"Erika's done this before. She overextends herself. You should all get to work and impress her when she comes back. She'd want you to take a risk. Once you face your worst fear, it will change your life forever. It will make every scene full of possibility and emotion. Once the impossible becomes possible . . . but I can tell by the look on your face you don't understand. So. Let me make this clear. It's the first assignment. Come back next week prepared to share your worst fear."

My stomach was flying down a cliff by the time he said "the first assignment." We'd use our worst fears as fuel for improvisation scenes. I didn't know what I was afraid of more. Hearing Osama's worst fear, or sharing mine out loud.


*Tuesday, September 13th*

On the bus home, Jason—funny he never spoke to me from grade six to eight but has suddenly become my best friend—said, "Mr. Beatty kicks ass."

I decided not to answer him. The exhaust behind the bus made a dark cloud outside the window. I couldn't wait to get home, call Morgan, and watch a funny movie.

"Miss Beatty's probably gone off to have a baby. Quiet like. Or maybe she's mentally ill and—"

"Can't you take a different bus home?"

"Isn't that what women *do* when they disappear?"

"Anybody ever call you LePage?"

He knew I was annoyed. "You need more sugar crisps in your morning. I'll get you some." He leaned so close I could hear the asthmatic rattle of his breath.

"You're wheezing in my face."

"You're worried about the first assignment. What are you scared of?"

"My basement." Oh shit. Why did I tell him? "The bogeyman. Being asked out by you. I agree with Osama. Why act out our real fears?"

"Because it's brilliant. Like he said, it's fuel. We'll have something to tap into in a play sometime. It's part of our training."

"I don't buy it."

"You're uptight. You'll never make it in drama."

Double shit. What if Jason's right?

Today Mr. Beatty started class with a confrontation. Osama had to share his worst fear or leave. *Salem alechem* to drama class.

I guessed how Osama felt. I live for drama. I've been dreaming about attending this high school for three years.

So Osama shared. His worst fear was awful. His mother had told him what it was like to watch a woman get stoned to death by the Taliban. He'd looked around the circle of our drama class and said, "My worst fear is that under your Canadian niceness, you hate Arabs. You hear my name and immediately think Osama bin Laden. You suspect I'm a terrorist. You could turn on me like that," he snapped his fingers.

Mr. Beatty left his director's chair and placed it in the middle of the circle for Osama to sit on. From the cupboard he brought out a box and walked around the inner circle offering each of us a beanbag from the box. At first no one took one.

"Did anyone in your family train in an Al-Qaeda camp?"

From the edge of the director's chair, Osama groaned. "Not this shit."

"Just play along with your worst fear, Osama. Humor us. It's a scene with fabulous potential. For the sake of the improvisation let's imagine someone in your family trained in an Al-Qaeda camp."

Osama's mouth twisted shut. Mr. Beatty walked slowly around the circle explaining the scenario. I couldn't believe it: one by one everyone in the circle took a beanbag. Not me. I sat on my hands.

"Remember 9/11. Innocent people on an ordinary work day in New York were targets. Think about it. Arab terrorists are planted all over North America. Look at Osama carefully. His family probably hates us. We're the West."

Osama started to protest but Mr. Beatty cut him off. "They're planning more events. Maybe Pearson Airport. Or Wonderland. Maybe this school."

I put my hands over my ears. I'd seen war movies about this. It was called fear-mongering. Only this time, instead of picking on Jews, it was Arabs. His lips kept moving, a machine gun of suspicions.

Rita threw the first beanbag. Me and my first impressions. WRONG!

Osama put his arms up to cover his head. One by one everyone started to pelt him. They stood up and yelled stuff at him. Terrorist! Murderer! Animal!

Osama fell over and lay tucked up in a fetal position. It was awful—was I the only one who didn't think he was acting?

Mr. Beatty removed his chair from the center of the circle and motioned for everyone to sit down. The bell rang. Mr. Beatty took out his marking folder and made marks beside our names. Then he asked us to go home and think about our worst fear for next class.

"People can be cruel," he said. "You need to understand every aspect of yourselves. The first assignment is all about emotion."

*Wednesday, September 14th, 4 p.m.*

Today I stood in the front hall a long time wondering what to do. Every day I come home and think someone's in the basement. It's so stupid. I decided to gather my courage and conquer my fear.

I opened the door and went down the stairs slowly. Each step creaked. Mousetraps sat along the basement wall—empty. I thought I heard something in the furnace room at the far end. I ran back upstairs to the kitchen for the sharp bread knife and the portable phone. I nearly threw up I was so scared. But I made myself go back down the stairs—twelve of them, I counted—across the cold, concrete floor, past the old sofa and the empty moving boxes to the furnace room. The big freezer left by the former owner sits beside the oil tank. It's the perfect size to hold a body. I closed my eyes and lifted the lid.

What an idiot I'm turning into. Under the mist were a few pizzas.

Fear is a stupid, stupid, stupid emotion.

*Thursday, September 15th*

At school today Michelle shared. Osama wasn't there—someone said he'd changed schools.

Michelle's fear was almost as scary as my basement.

"My dad's a pilot," she said. "Every Saturday he bugs me to go to Buttonville Airport with him. He teaches skydiving and wants me to try it."

She stopped talking. Her eyes were little white parachutes in her face.

Mr. Beatty put his chair in the middle and motioned for her to come forward.

"It's a scary thought. Jumping out of a plane and relying on something in your backpack to save you."

"Yeah."

Rita—maybe she's out to be teacher's pet—said, "I heard somewhere there are more accidents skydiving than on the road."

"It's the thought of my parachute not working that scares me."

Mr. Beatty patted Michelle on the shoulder. "Thank you for having such courage. For today's improv I want everyone to lie on the floor while Michelle helps us imagine her worst fear."

Michelle sat on the director's chair, her eyes closed, and began talking. Mr. Beatty came and stood right beside me with the marking folder, so I had to lie down and close my eyes too. It was quit or go along.

Michelle said we were jumping out of the plane at an altitude of 13,500 feet. We were floating, free-falling REALLY FAST. A cold wind whipped by noisily at 120 miles per hour. We pulled a cord and felt the tug of the small chute, the drogue, as it deployed. It would keep us from going any faster. Above us we saw the drogue puffed up like a big beach ball. Below us, through white clouds, the earth was out of focus, a blur of dark colors.

It was time to deploy the main chute. It would slow us down to a safe, leisurely twenty-five miles per hour. Tug on the ripcord at our waist. No jerk. We looked up to see only the drogue. The main parachute hadn't deployed. Tug again. Fumble around with both hands. Tug. Tug. We were passing through a cloud. The end of the cord was securely in our hand. Was it stuck? We came out of the cloud and saw the earth below us now, alarmingly close. Tug again. The main chute was not going to deploy. Details of the earth came into focus. Brown fields. Green lumpy trees. Frantic fumbling. The earth was coming closer and closer. You could see a pond and a tractor moving across a field.

It was so real, I flapped my arms, trying to fly.

Michelle screamed. Me too! I hit the earth like a fly on a windshield. Blood everywhere.

After class, I avoided LePage. Everybody was saying how great it was to be so terrified, but I felt sick. I waited in the girls' washroom, getting up my nerve.

*Friday, September 16th*

At home. Alone. Listening. The first assignment has unleashed horrible thoughts. There's a nutcase waiting in the basement, waiting to take me off somewhere and chop me up alive, limb by limb.

How do I explain *that* to Mom? I'm supposed to be mature and independent and I feel like a two-year-old, terrified of our basement.

Today I ordered myself to face my fear. No calling Morgan. I opened the door to the basement, holding the big bread knife. I heard the creaks as I moved down the stairs, stopping on each one. Ahead I saw the empty moving boxes and the old sofa. Empty mousetraps. Nothing else. When I reached the last step I heard the soft whoosh of the freezer door shutting. Freaky.

There couldn't be anyone . . . could there? And if there was? I took several deep breaths.

"Who's there?"

Not a sound. I wanted this over and done with. I hated this fear thing. I moved toward the furnace room. Behind me I thought I heard something. The scrape of a cardboard box? Was someone in one of the boxes?

I kicked them. One after the other. The boxes were empty. It was my imagination. My fear breathing.

I was trembling, but I went into the furnace room. I stared at the freezer a long time. I whipped around and stared at the empty boxes.

I counted out loud to ten. Even my voice shook. I had to do it. I opened the freezer.

No dead body. What did I expect? A severed head?

Under the mist there were two pizzas.

My fear of the basement is ridiculous. I'm going to conquer it.

(If you're looking for the bread knife, Mom, I left it under the sofa cushion . . . just in case).

*Monday, September 19th, 4 p.m.*

*Trying to be brave. In basement alone. So scared I can hardly write.*

*Jason phoned yesterday. Something terrible was on news. A skydiving accident at Buttonville Airport. Victim's parachute didn't open—*

*A BOX IS MOVING!!!*

My heart's still pounding. I'm back upstairs, locked in bathroom with the phone and my diary. Shit. Did a box move or did I imagine it? I should have brought the knife with me. This assignment is freaking me out. I don't hear a thing through the door. Morgan better get here soon.

What about the accident on the news? It could have been anybody.

"I bet it's Michelle." Jason's exact words. Why'd he say that? Is fear taking over his imagination too? Hundreds of people skydive at Buttonville. Does he know something?

Michelle wasn't at school today. Creepy coincidence? Couldn't she be sick? If she doesn't show up by Wednesday for drama, then I'll suspect it's her too. Then I'll be suspicious of everyone in drama class: Jason (he called me with the news) and Rita (she goes along with this stuff too easily); even Mr. Beatty (he's directing these improvs).

Doorbell. Why do I feel braver with Morgan here?

*Wednesday, Sept. 21st, 5 pm. Waiting Room of St. Joseph's Hospital*

Mr. Beatty dressed up as Miss Beatty. Talk about weird. He wore high heels and black leather and an amazing wig. It looked like Miss Beatty's hair, maybe shorter, but same red streaks. He even had red lips, but when he spoke, it was *his* voice.

"I have bad news about Michelle," he said, then told us what we already knew. "The parachutes were kept in an unsecured locker. The police aren't releasing any more information until further notice."

"Why are you dressed up like your sister?" Rita said.

He switched to a high voice. He even had that faint English accent. It sounded just like Miss Beatty.

"What makes you so sure I'm not Miss Beatty," he—she—said, sitting on the director's chair, legs crossed.

Freaky. *Who* was sitting on that chair?

"Wow. You're fantastic," Rita said.

Rita and I are definitely NOT part of the same human race. I started wondering: had it been Miss Beatty all along? Or was Mr. Beatty cross-dressing, acting like her, trying to win our trust as *her?* It was a crazy-maker.

I thought about leaving the class, right then and there, but I was mesmerized by the person in the chair. I decided to stay long enough to figure everything out and then quit. Jason was right. I'd never get past the first assignment. Theater wasn't for me.

Jason stopped coughing to ask, "How do you know it's Michelle?"

You could have heard a fly leave a window it was so quiet.

"Really, Jason. Don't you suspect it's Michelle? It's such horrible timing."

Instinctively I held my chest, remembering hitting the earth in the improv. Some kids looked upset. A few shook their heads, not wanting to believe Michelle was dead.

Our teacher stared at us. "Would anyone like to call Michelle's family and find out for sure?"

No one moved. What would you say? "Hello . . . is Michelle still alive?"

"Imagine it was Michelle. Imagine she faced her fear with us last week. It's empowering to conquer it. Be as brave as Michelle. Who's willing to give us a scene for an improv today?"

No one moved.

"Do it for Michelle."

Not a breath taken, except a wheezy one by Jason.

She—he—the teacher stared at me, eyes like empty boxes.

"Do it for your craft."

Was it Miss Beatty? I wanted it to be her. I wanted badly for everything to be normal, to be in the best drama program ever, to get over my fear of my basement.

"I'm afraid . . ." I said. "After school . . . before my mom gets home. I'm alone."

There. I'd almost said it. No one laughed. My words had little drogues on them floating through the air above our drama circle. The blood in my veins rushed out my feet—they felt numb, sawed off by a sharp knife—while the rest of me was free-falling in fearland.

"A common fear," said our teacher. "One I had myself as a child. The basement's a dark place, with too many places for someone to hide. We used to play there."

The director's chair was put in the center of the circle. Everyone waited for me to come forward. I couldn't have moved if there'd been a knife at my throat.

I didn't have to. Jason coughed, then said, "I was hoping to share mine. Get it over with. My asthma's bad this time of year—"

Jason stopped to cough. His lungs sounded full of fluid.

Our teacher stared from Jason, to me, then back to Jason. "All right, Jason. Let's explore yours first."

Jason coughed his way over to the chair.

"Have you got a puffer?"

Jason reached in his pocket and pulled out his puffer, put it to his mouth, but the Beatty person took it and click-clacked on those high heels over to an open window. I noticed how thick the calves were. A man's calves? But a girl's could look like that too. Calf muscles bulged in high heels.

"Ventolin opens the passageways in your lungs. Is it scary to think of your asthma getting so bad you can't breathe?"

Jason nodded, coughing again.

"Try to relax with this one, okay? We'll do a little improv around you."

Rita was called and given the puffer with instructions to act like a homeopathic guru. From there things went crazy. Rita got into the role. Really into it. She launched into a tirade about healthy bodies, vitamins and minerals supporting the lungs, how Jason should abstain from medications that made his body a slave to the chemical industry. She threw the puffer out the window. Jason freaked out and tried to leave the class. Rita barred the door. Everybody took sides, screaming at each other. Miss or Mr. Beatty picked up the marking folder and wrote stuff down.

I didn't join the "improv." Jason sank to the floor. He was choking on his coughing. When he threw up I knew I had to do something. I ran to the phone at the back of the class and dialed 911.

Now Jason's in an oxygen tent at St. Joseph's Hospital. They won't let me see him until tomorrow. Miss Beatty, whatever, tried to see him but they won't let her in either. Good. She let it get out of hand. Thank God he's alive.

*Thursday, September 23rd, 3p.m.*

I'm writing this outside drama. I can hear the click clack of high heels around the improv circle. Probably apologizing. I don't care who's teaching that class. I quit.

I'm going to the office to withdraw. As of tomorrow I'm going to North Toronto with Morgan. I'm not cut out for drama. I never got past the first assignment.

I'll visit Jason before going home.

When I get home, if I hear anything in the basement, if I hear anything anywhere, I'll ignore it. I'll call Morgan to come watch a movie. I'll go down to the freezer and get us a pizza.

THERE IS NOTHING IN THE BASEMENT.

*Thursday, September 23rd, 4:30*
*So wrong*
*the director's chair—in the basement!*
*scared*
*noises overhead*
*knife gone!*
*hiding this journal — please come home Mom*
*click clack—first stair*
*love you*

## X X X X X

*Anne Laurel Carter was born in Don Mills where she learned to fear basements. She left Don Mills at seventeen to work on a cow farm in Israel, then an antique store in California, before returning to Toronto to become a teacher. Most characters in her novels and short stories are inspired by real events and people. She has won the Mr. Christie Award for* Under a Prairie Sky *and the Canadian Library Association Book of the Year Award for Children for* Last Chance Bay. *Among her published books are* No Missing Parts *(Red Deer, 2002) and* My Home Bay *(Red Deer, 2003).*

# PRINCE SANDRED THE SILENT:
## A TRULY GRIM TALE

### Priscilla Galloway

"**S**andred, drop that snake at once."

"But Mother, that's Sam. Sam's my favorite snake in the whole world."

"Best let the little prince keep his pet, your majesty. He threw such a tantrum last week, I thought he'd choke."

"Go choke yourself. You burned Sam's old skin. Bad Thalia. I hate you."

I let my eyes rest on Thalia, my nurse. She looked away. They always looked away. The queen, my mother, was no different. People told me I was handsome, but they always looked away.

Sam felt cool and dry. He rustled. He curled around my arm under my sweater. I didn't like noisy things, or hot things, or things that yip and bite. Sam smelled good, musty a bit. His old skin was transparent, translucent, shining when the sun caught it like a jeweled rope. Diamond beads glittered around the eyeholes. "Nasty thing," Thalia shuddered. She put on a glove to pick up her trophy, Sam's discarded skin. She threw the glove on the fire afterwards.

"I should take a piece of your skin to make up for Sam's," I told Thalia, "but your skin isn't pretty."

I could have had her skin, not the whole of it maybe, but certainly a piece. My father had been king for thirty years. He could do what he wanted. Within limits, he would do what I wanted. Flayed Thalia. Ha! But I didn't want her skin, not then, when I was a child.

While he was alive, Sam often slithered away from me. It was better when he died. His skin was still cool and dry, and I could easily curl him around my neck. I liked the way he began to smell—sweet, though not like lilies.

There were lilies when Aunt Augusta died. They put her in a big wooden box on top of a table in the great hall. Mother lifted me up to see. I put out my hand and touched Aunt Augusta's face. She felt cold and firm. She was rather squishy before.

"Kiss her," somebody said, and I bent my lips to hers. They felt cool and firm. They tasted a bit like raspberries. For the first time ever, I was looking at Aunt Augusta and her tongue was not wagging at both ends, as Mother used to say. The quiet was profound and redolent of peace.

When Thalia found Sam's dead body, she was ready to throw it on the fire, just like the skin. My father stopped her. He said he'd help me bury the body under the linden tree. "A royal funeral," he laughed. I wanted to keep Sam more than anything else in the world. I didn't ever want to bury him. However, my father got his way.

When I was nine, my parents hired Perceval to be my tutor. Thalia left. She had found my dead frogs. The box didn't smell much as long as it was closed, but Thalia rebelled. I readily persuaded Father to let her go. Poor foolish Thalia, deprived of serving me!

Perceval was an immense improvement. "I see how much you love the little things," he said. "You like exploring them. You need formaldehyde, Sandred. And dissecting knives."

Did he tell my father anything? No doubt the king wanted me to develop my talents. Perceval put in a huge order at the Chemists' and Alchemists' Emporium. Jars, bottles, rubber corks. Various powders and liquids. I hunted fresh frogs and immersed them in the different preservatives, testing their properties. From then on, I spent my days in the lab. I could have a frog opened up and pinned back, all layers and organs exposed, in forty-five seconds. I learned to deal quick death, snapping the neck or inserting a slim knife at the top of the spine. Snakes, mice, squirrels, cats came to my dissecting table. At last, a wriggly puppy was stilled by my loving hands.

Tiny blood vessels, exquisite small muscles, the pinkness of fresh bone: how beautiful they were. I became a connoisseur of death.

Official functions saw me no more. The robes of office, sable and ermine, the gold chain with the great seal, the heir's coronet itself were handed to my younger brother. He likes playing Prince.

Retirement from the official role has made it easier for me to go away to study. The University of Salerno in Italy has long been famous for its medical school. One of my teachers there was Trotula, famous the world over for diagnosing and curing problems of pregnancy and childbirth. We are forbidden to perform autopsies, although Trotula says a physician can understand the living only by examining the dead. Publicly, she obeys the church. She is no doubt unwilling to be burned alive for heresy.

Customs differ wherever one goes. Some things can be done here in Italy that could not even be suggested in my native land. For example, I have obtained three fetuses, two extremely tiny, with huge heads, but one almost babe-sized. They swim pallidly in great, glass jars. They never cry. Sometimes I take out my dead babies and stroke their satin skin. I kiss their bodies with closed lips, which I then carefully wash. Afterwards, my lips burn and tingle. More than anything else in the world I long to penetrate dead bodies, to lay bare their muscles, their organs, their very bones. This is the greatest intimacy of all.

Once Perceval brought me for my pleasure a young woman. She was alive. Did Perceval not know that I prefer clay-cold, unyielding skin? The perfume of lilies and formaldehyde excites my senses. Silence is my sound. Enraged, I hit the damsel with the flat of my hand. Red color bloomed in her face and she cried out, a sharp, short cry. She bared her back and handed me a knotted scourge.

Furious, I threw it down. "Am I a monster, to torture a woman?" I demanded. "Begone." My hands thought of her neck and how she would feel when she became silent and cool. Desire flamed through me, and I held back my hands with difficulty. How I would adore her when she lay flaccid, open to my knives. My hands reached out, reached, and drew back. I marveled, understanding in that instant what I truly am. I am a man like other men: I desire women. I can love their bodies. I can love their inmost selves.

Perceval made an arrangement with a coffin maker. I paid the death merchant for night hours with the dear corpses, my body learning their bodies, their smooth, soft faces, their silent mouths. At funerals, I gazed long upon each corpse; soundlessly, I communed with the dead. In the summer the smell of lilies mingled with the sick-sweet smell of decay: my aphrodisiac.

Once there was a great fire. Fifty blackened cadavers waited on trestles in the cathedral while relatives wept, screamed, or fainted, finding their own. Strolling among the bodies, I drank in the sweet scent of charred and rotting flesh.

I too swooned once. "Alas, poor sir, have you found one dear to you?" sighed the young maid who chafed my cold hands. I could not tell her that in my eyes and in my nose, under my hands and in my ears, every one of them was indeed most dear. That afternoon, I claimed two of the charred corpses and had them borne away.

Late at night, Perceval helped carry my prizes to the great cellar. I had thought to lie there with them before beginning with my knives, and had a bed made ready. Alas, this delight was denied me. The fire had had them first. Blistered skin, baked flesh, fell away at my gentlest touch. I obtained two long porcelain tubs and laid a body in each, bestowing a warm kiss on each pair of blistered lips before filling their bath with preservative. A huge marble slab served as a table on which to lay the bodies and explore with my sharp knives what changes fire had wrought.

My servants began to leave me on short notice. Although I doubled and tripled the wages of their replacements, none stayed for more than a few nights. Perceval relayed to me the local gossip about our establishment. I was not surprised; little people possess small minds.

A month later, a neighbor's child disappeared. Perceval heard that all buildings were to be searched. It was only too easy to guess that mine would be first. In that instance, suspicion was misplaced. I am not a fool, so to draw upon myself the attention of the law. Nonetheless, my home would hardly bear a systematic inspection.

Raging, I abandoned all my specimens, the work of years. I saved only my knives as Perceval and I took horse and spurred to the east. Then I blessed my father's money which provided fleet Arab steeds for both of us. I blessed my princely training. Warm animals were always abhorrent, but as a child I was forced to ride, becoming a good horseman despite myself. Although I had seldom ridden since coming to Italy, I found myself steady in the saddle, using reins and whip with ease.

East we went, Perceval and I. In the beginning, bereavement gnawed. All my loves were lost. It was May, however, and the sun was warm. We rode into lands of legend and enchantment. Surely I could build a castle hereabout. In the center, a keep would rise with dungeons below and a high tower atop. If the keep was walled, I could even have windows in the stone and daylight shining on a new marble slab. I have longed to be able to work, and to love, by the light of the sun.

For two days we rode through dark forest. Vast trees groaned in winds far above us, but Perceval and I rode below in stillness and gloom. At the edge of the forest we forded a wide, swirling river. Perceval was almost swept away, but I exerted my strength and held his horse. It found its footing again, and so did he. This was fortunate, as he was carrying most of my knives. The loss would have been great.

We struggled up a steep bank into a meadow of green hay where we hobbled our horses and threw ourselves down to rest. Hardly had our eyes closed when we heard a splashing in the river and hoofbeats drawing near. Three riders advanced upon us. All were armed in black, without emblazonment. They rode black steeds. Two of them rode with drawn swords, while the foremost whirled a spiked ball around his head.

Perceval sprang up, clutching his sword and running forward to seize the bridle of the first attacker. I snatched up my brand no less hastily. The ball caught Perceval's arm, and his weapon fell. He kept his grip upon the horse's bridle, however, and the animal reared, throwing its rider to the ground. I was not slow to pierce his neck, and saw his red blood pumping fiercely onto the emerald meadow, running down into the black earth. I might come to like this knight greatly later, when he was cold and stiff.

But there was little time for these thoughts. Perceval's arm hung useless, and two riders with naked swords continued their advance.

Sometimes a fighter may seem valorous when he is merely desperate. I hamstrung one fellow's horse. As it stumbled, I pulled the rider off balance and with one blow separated his head from his shoulders. At that, the third man turned to flee. I cut the hobbles on my horse and leapt into the saddle, racing after him.

At the edge of a thicket of thorns I caught the miscreant and toppled him from his steed, raising my sword for the fatal blow. "Mercy," he cried. "Hear my tale and make your fortune. Let me tell you of the dead maiden and the prophecy."

My ears prickled; my sword arm fell harmless to my side. "Dead maiden?" I croaked.

"Aye," gasped the dead man, not yet clay-cold and silent. "She is dead but does not decay. People have talked of little else for a month now. Her dwarfs mourn her night and day. We were on our way to take her from them. She is a princess, with great wealth. There is a prophecy, a kiss to be given."

"Be silent, churl, how dare you speak of kissing the dead!" My sword pierced his throat and the bright blood bubbled. He continued to mouth words, but no sound came from his lips except the gurgle of his death.

I salved and bound Perceval's arm before getting out my knives. In ecstasy, I explored heads and bodies, drinking the smell and feel of death in the green meadow on that sweet spring day. How sad that I had neither a scale to weigh nor calipers to measure their various anatomies, let alone jars and preservatives. What a waste!

Even as I fondled and cut those male bodies, however, an image of the dead maiden formed and grew. My perfect love, dead and not decaying! My passion has never found its ideal object: one whose dear, dead flesh will remain always cool and firm to my touch, who will have no breath to displease with taint of garlic or onion, who will keep forever the musty-sweet odor that my nostrils crave. Like other men, I yearn for lasting love.

Daylight must have been fading for some time without my noticing. By the time I roused myself, it was almost night. Our attackers had approached like brigands, but they were accoutered like people of importance, and their information made it likely they lived not far away. Reluctantly, I realized the bodies must be hidden from those who might come to search. Perceval had already recognized the need. Despite his injured arm, he had scouted the thicket and found an old quarry. Its stone walls rose smooth, moss-covered, high. At the bottom, green scum covered stagnant water. One by one, I draped the bodies over a horse and brought them to the edge.

With their horses' bridles, I tied the heavy sword to each corpse. I weighted their leather jerkins with stones. One by one, I rolled them over. Perceval helped. The injured horse followed its master.

Perceval and I were both exhausted by the time this task was completed. We made a light meal of bread and cheese, the last of the rations we had brought, and slept in our cloaks. In the morning we washed in the river and changed our stained garments. I was forced to wear rich clothes, suitable enough for a prince, but not at all suitable for a traveler. Unfortunately, in the haste of my departure, I had brought no others. White satin, pearl-embroidered, and a cloak of scarlet would have to suffice until I could purchase sober jerkin and hose.

The morning was again sunny and warm, and we rode on cheerily enough, although a certain pall hung over me. Did the dead maiden even exist? In the dusk I had almost touched her, so real she seemed. By day, I believed no longer. And even if she existed, what chance had I of finding her?

Birds sang as we ambled on, however, and presently we came to a thatched cottage by the road. It seemed a modest dwelling, built lower than most. In search of food and drink, Perceval knocked at the blue-painted door. No reply. He knocked again. Silence.

Then I heard or thought I heard a sound of weeping. Perceval raised his head. It seemed he had heard it too. He gestured, and I led the way around the building, following a tidy flagstone path between flowerbeds overflowing with garish scarlet blooms. As we rounded the house, the weeping became louder.

We beheld a bier covered with a rich golden cloak. On it lay unmoving a damsel clothed in white heavily embroidered in gold thread, almost a match for my own attire. I dismounted and approached, my eyes fixed on the maiden. People scattered in front of me. All was silent.

My heart thudded noisily as I came near to that pale face, whiter than her dress. My hand touched her forehead: clay-cold. Her hair lay in raven ringlets about her face. Her eyes were closed. Her mouth curved in livid bows, pulling my own down, as if to a magnet. My perfect love. My mate. I pressed my lips to hers. My arm passed under her shoulders and raised the lifeless body to my breast. Ah! I itched to possess her, to love her with my body and my knives.

But what do I feel? Is there a stir, a shudder throughout her frame? Slowly the lids rise, and eyes of deepest blue meet mine. Around me the air bursts with noise.

The face is no longer clay-cold, the lips no longer gloriously livid. She coughs and chokes in a most unseemly way. I draw back in revulsion as little men press around her, weeping and laughing, pulling at her hands, touching her hair.

Disgusting! Never have I been so deceived! Perceval holds my horse. I mount and we ride away. I hear in the distance a cry of, "My prince," and we put our horses to the gallop. What an ugly voice she has. So loud.

## X X X X X

*Priscilla Galloway has been a full-time author since 1993.* Too Young to Fight: Memories from our Youth During World War II, *won the major*

---

*international Bologna Ragazzi award in 2000, the first Canadian book to do so. Other titles among her twenty-two books were nominated for the Canadian Library Association, the Mr. Christie's, and Red Cedar awards. Previously, Galloway taught in high schools and universities and was a language arts consultant. She was honored as Teacher of the Year by the Ontario Council of Teachers of English. She is a past president of CANSCAIP (the Canadian Society of Children's Authors, Illustrators and Performers). Priscilla's eclectic career also includes operating a trailer park and managing an apartment building, not to mention a brief foray into cosmetic sales and a short stint as a cucumber farmer. Born in Montreal in 1930, Priscilla has lived, written, taught, and scuba-dived from Pacific to Atlantic, from southern farming country to northern mines, from the Caribbean to New Zealand. Her home base is Toronto. Readers must decide if she is really "a mixture of Lucille Ball and Vincent Price."*

# Apollo and Dionysos

## William Bell

"Pathetic," Daniel muttered as he glowered out the Airbus window at a bunch of olive-clad men pushing a wheeled staircase toward the still moving jet. "The second biggest city in the country and they don't even have a proper air terminal."

The flight had been a three-and-a-half-hour misery. Inedible food, dry, stale air scraping away at his bronchial tubes, and a plane full of holiday cheer types reveling at their escape from ice and snow.

"We're here!" his mother announced, running a comb though her hair.

"Finally," his father smiled. Daniel rolled his eyes. Yes, wonderful, he said to himself. Cuba. For two months.

His parents, both doctors, were part of some kind of medical exchange program—Daniel didn't know and could have cared less about the details—and would give talks and study and tour and "network" and do all the other academic things they were so fond of. Daniel, dragged along for his health as well as the "educational experience," had not been allowed to stay home. His acceptance into the university classical music program had already been granted—two years earlier than normal. Missing forty days of school posed no threat. His principal at the Caledonia Music Academy had enthusiastically endorsed a leave of absence for Daniel.

The plane lurched to a halt, and the tourists heaved themselves from their seats, jamming the aisle, reaching up to the overhead compartments for their cabin baggage, chattering excitedly about snorkeling, sunbathing, dance classes, and Spanish lessons by the pool.

Daniel waited until the clogged aisle began to clear, then retrieved his backpack and followed his parents to the door.

A blaze of sunlight, violent in its intensity, greeted him at the top of the stairs. The air was thick with humidity and the odor of vegetation and diesel fuel. Squinting, Daniel walked across the tarmac, baked by the shimmering heat that rose in waves from the ground. Inside the terminal, an air conditioning duct pumped damp moldy air into the room. Daniel could practically feel malignant microbes floating around him. He joined the line for the passport check, his mother's forced good cheer as irritating as the thought of the forty-five minute bus ride to the resort in Bacanao National Park.

The streets of Santiago de Cuba, Daniel observed from the coach window, were narrow and dusty. There were no lawns around the small concrete dwellings, not much in the way of gardens. In the outskirts, scrawny goats and chickens stood behind makeshift fences of wire, board, and cactus. At every intersection, it seemed, men and women and children stood chatting, apparently waiting for rides.

"Doesn't anybody in this place have a job?" Daniel asked himself. As the city dropped away behind the bus, the road twisted and turned through the foothills of the Sierra Maestras. Yellow earth, palms, banana trees; steep hillsides, rocky gullies, dry riverbeds; concrete shacks with corrugated iron roofs. Shoeless kids, mangy dogs, women leaning in doorways looking out at the road.

At last the ocean appeared. Mountains, purpled by haze, seemed to leap into the afternoon sky. With a chirp and a hiss of air brakes, the bus pulled into Club Los Amigos. Three star rating. Out of a possible five.

Daniel heaved a sigh.

x x x x x

Daniel's room was cramped and sparsely equipped. A small desk, on which his laptop sat open. A TV whose screen was smaller than his computer's; nothing on anyway. The workers had removed one of the single beds and set up a table. It now held Daniel's electronic practice keyboard, a sheet music file alphabetically arranged by composer, his books, carefully aligned between two bookends, a stack of DVD movies (laid out in a clear plastic box in the order in which he intended to view them, having planned it so that he could watch one every three days until the ordeal of the trip was over), his CDs (data and music), his asthma puffers. In his closet he had hung his clothes, grouped by categories: T-shirts, short-sleeved shirts, long-sleeved shirts, trousers. His underwear and handkerchiefs were folded and neatly stowed in drawers. His shoes were neatly arranged on the floor.

He had his own bathroom, with a dripping tap, a shower stall with a torn plastic curtain, a sink with one glass shelf barely large enough to accommodate his medications and the stack of aromatic non-allergenic soap bars he had brought from home. Each morning someone made his bed, shaping his towels into swans, and tidied.

Daniel's parents were gone most of the day and sometimes evenings. They worked in Santiago, taking a taxi to and fro. Daniel practiced in the mornings, read or did logic and math puzzles in his room, occasionally ventured onto the white sand beach, the only person there in long pants, long-sleeved shirt, and wide-brimmed hat. His mother warned him each morning about the sun. "You'll burn to a cinder in no time," she predicted, always including a word on the virtues of sunblock.

x x x x x

The resort consisted of a dozen two-story buildings set around a pool and landscaped grounds with grass, palmettos, and bougainvillea hedges tumbling with pink and purple blossoms. The shore was minutes away, offering a bit of shade under trees whose names Daniel could only guess at, assuming he was interested. The beach bar seemed always to be busy, the speakers hung under the thatched roof booming salsa music.

Daniel hated salsa.

The food at the buffet was terrible. Meat and more meat. Rice, with meat. Soup, with meat. Fish. Pasta with meat sauce. A vegetarian, Daniel would have to subsist on bread and salads and omelets.

There were only a few people his age at the resort, mostly girls, all giggles and vanity. They strutted around, shoulders back, yearning to be ogled. The guys seemed intent on drinking and smoking as much as they could before they fell over.

As he passed the beach volleyball net on his second day at Los Amigos, he was hailed by a woman's voice. "Hey, man! You play?"

All seven young men and women were tanned and toned, their limbs glowing with oil. Daniel, garbed from head to foot to keep away the sun, muttered, "No thanks."

"Come on, man, we need a fourth," insisted a sinewy black youth who tossed the ball casually from hand to hand. "Strip down and join us."

One of the other men said something in Spanish and the women laughed.

"I'm asthmatic. I don't play sports," Daniel said as he trudged through the deep sand. "Besides, I've got better things to do."

As if the Hades in which he was exiled for sixty days was not enough, Daniel found that each time he entered the gallery that led to his room, a blur streaked from beneath a rattan couch, snarling and snapping. A small, terrier-like dog with a patch of bare skin in the center of its back would stalk him, its ears flat against its head, lips curled to reveal menacing teeth. Heart pounding, Daniel would walk backwards to his door, and escape inside.

× × × × ×

Daniel alternated between his preference for Mozart ("So serene," he told his father once), and Bach ("So logical."). One morning, he was practicing a piano version of Mozart's Adagio from the Clarinet Concerto in A. He wore earphones, but the drone of the air conditioner intruded like a bad smell. He was interrupted by a knock on the door.

"It's me, dear."

Daniel rose and unlocked the door. "What are you doing back so soon?" he asked his mother.

"The hosts at the university have laid on a tour of Santiago for us," she complained. "One of those social obligations. They insisted that you come along. Your father is waiting for us in Cespedes Park, in front of the cathedral."

"I'm not really—"

"You have to go," she cut in. "It would be rude not to. Besides," she added without conviction, "it's a very historic city."

"I'm sure."

"Well, with hundreds of years to work on it, they must have come up with something interesting," she said.

Four hours later, having suffered the ancient casa in Cespedes Park, the cathedral (where Daniel and his parents muttered about superstition and ignorance), three museums, an art gallery, two plazas baking under the afternoon sun, the rum factory, a factory where men and women sat behind tables rolling cigars while a woman on a stool read stories to them over a loud speaker—after consuming a number of large bottles of *agua minerale*, Daniel followed his parents and the guide from the university to a graveyard.

The Cemeterio Santa Ifigena was, Daniel's father promised, their last stop. Daniel trailed behind his parents and their host, Dr. Mendez, past a pond in the shape of a cross. Narrow sidewalks flanked by flowerbeds ran between marble graves adorned with statuary depicting angels, crosses, and saints, and surrounded by wrought iron fences. The sturdy monuments had been built above ground. The thought of being literally surrounded by decaying corpses made Daniel wince. In spite of himself, he shuddered as a phrase he had once heard slipped into his mind: city of the dead. But he caught himself. Stupid, he thought. Unreasonable.

"And this way," Dr. Mendez rambled on, "is the tomb of one of our national heroes, Jose Marti." He led Daniel's parents toward a large octagonal mausoleum.

Daniel hung back. The others were soon out of sight behind the graves. He took a path toward an area where the tombs were less overpowering—simple structures skirted with clean gravel, a few ornamented with baskets of flowers. He found himself by a low iron fence marking the cemetery's border. On the other side, dry brown grass patched the bare ground between thorny shrubs. Cicadas thrummed rhythmically in the hot, still air. Below the cicadas' song, Daniel heard someone keening tunelessly. He scanned the desolate area beyond the fence. Almost out of sight behind a bush, a figure knelt, her back to him, before a fire of paper trash and twigs. Daniel heard a faint ching-ching along with the chanting. The figure moved, tossing something into the flames. Ching-ching. She wore a soiled white shirt. Bare soles poked out from beneath a dark skirt. Her voice was thin and dry. He didn't understand the words, but knew they were not Spanish. The singer poured something onto the fire and the flames brightened. She repeated a single word five or six times, then fell silent.

More superstition, Daniel muttered. Stupid nonsense.

The chanter's shoulders stiffened. Her back straightened. She rose slowly and, just as slowly, turned to face Daniel. She was old, rail thin, her skin like coal. A red bandana covered her head, and brass hoops hung from earlobes that framed a skeletal face, the skin taut over her cheekbones. Copper bracelets adorned skinny wrists. In her claw-like hands she held a leather pouch.

Her piercing black eyes smoldered malevolently. Daniel felt an icy finger jab his spine as she bared her teeth. He took a step back as she reached into the bag—ching-ching—and withdrew it, then, with an almost casual flick of her wrist—ching!—flung something at him.

Too late, Daniel threw up a hand. Something sharp pinched the soft vee of flesh beneath his adam's apple. He sucked in his breath. He took a step back, stumbled on the edge of the sidewalk, and fell. He scrambled to his feet. Like a crow, the small dark figure drifted away through the trees, leaving the fire burning. Daniel's hand rose to his throat, felt something hard there, stuck in his skin. He pulled it away, crying out at the burning pain. It looked like a claw, no larger than the end of his little finger. Shreds of fur clung to the base. Disgusted, he threw it aside. He spit on his hands, rubbed them together, dried them on his trousers. He rubbed his throat with his handkerchief. It came away with only a tiny smear of blood.

"Daniel!" His father's voice.

"Coming," Daniel called out. "Be right there!" He trotted back toward the cross-shaped pond and found his parents and their escorts.

"Where were you?" his mother asked, dabbing her damp forehead with a silk scarf.

"I got lost."

"Well, it's time we went back to the hotel. You look pale, dear. The heat must be getting to you."

"Yeah, maybe," Daniel said.

"I'm afraid your father and I have to spend the next three days or so here in Santiago," his mother told him. "Another request to report on our research. We'll be so busy it makes no sense to run back and forth between the city and the hotel."

Daniel nodded absently, looking back over his shoulder.

✕ ✕ ✕ ✕ ✕

The next morning, Daniel awoke with a fever scratching at his throat and a throbbing in his temples. By lunchtime his aching bones seemed to have filled with cement. After pulling the drapes across the patio door and turning up the air conditioner, he padded to the bathroom, swallowed some pills, and took to his bed. He opened a book but couldn't concentrate. He listened to his portable CD player but, after a while, flung it aside. Then he drifted into a hot and sweaty sleep.

In a dream, he lay naked on a cold marble slab, surrounded by gravestones, silhouetted against a full moon. Although he was sick with fear, he had the sense that he belonged there. He heard insects stirring in the grass around the slab, and the soft footfalls of larger creatures stalking between the monuments. A dark shape loomed high above him, wavering like a kite, intermittently blocking the moon's cold silver light. Slowly, implacably, the shape descended, growing larger and gradually acquiring shape. Something familiar came into focus. It was the leathery face of the woman he had seen the day before, dark cavities where her eyes should have been. She grimaced, revealing stumpy, yellow teeth. She reached out to gather him to her. Ching-ching. Cold, bony arms clutched him, tighter and tighter, until his chest was crushed. He gasped and struggled for breath.

"No!" he begged, "no!"

Daniel awoke in the grip of a full-scale asthma attack. His lungs seemed collapsed within his aching chest. He crawled, wheezing, to the edge of his bed. Fell to the floor. Pulled himself to his feet. One. After. Another. Fumbled in the dark for his puffer. Jammed it in his mouth. Plunged-and-sucked. Sat down, willing himself to fight the instinct to gasp for breath, staring at the crack between the drapes where welcome amber light from the lamps on the grounds seeped through.

After a while, his breathing restored to normal, he went into the bathroom and gulped down half a bottle of water. In the harsh glow of the fluorescent light over the mirror he noticed a tiny scab on his throat in the center of a patch of angry red skin. It was itchy. Infected, he thought, reaching for his first aid kit.

x x x x x

Daniel kept to his bed for two days, snapping at the maid when she tried to enter, taking no food, only bottled water, fighting off nightmares and the constricting vise of his disease, oscillating wildly between terror and relief.

On the third day, the day his parents were to return, he drifted into wakefulness and got out of bed. It was noon. Standing in the shower, he vigorously rinsed away the sweat and bad dreams. He toweled off, looked in the mirror. The mark on his neck was gone. He grinned at his reflection. "That's better," he said.

× × × × ×

That night, in Daniel's dream, stars sparked in the sky above a calm dark ocean. A powerful animal sprinted along a beach, breathing effortlessly, awash in night odors—the salt sea, fish, the dewy ground that skirted the beach, the blossoms in the hedges. Overhead, Daniel hovered like a kite. He saw the bones and sinews and muscles ripple beneath the creature's skin, felt the heat rising from its back. The beast was indistinct, a shape only, but Daniel felt its power, its joy as it ran. It swerved inland, crossed a dirt road, slipped into the trees as it headed into the mountains. Daniel soared higher, followed the shape as it disappeared, then reappeared under the trees. Then he veered off, banking like a glider, and the dream dissolved.

Daniel awoke to birdcalls outside his patio door. He stretched languidly, hopped out of bed, drew the curtain aside. Workers with machetes, chatting amiably in Spanish, were cutting the grass between the palmettos and bougainvillea shrubs. The pleasant memory of his dream faded like smoke in a breeze. He showered, took his medications, sauntered out into the morning. At the end of the hall, the little mongrel darted from under the couch and clamped his jaws, snarling, on Daniel's pant leg. He bent over and clouted the mangy animal on its head. The dog released its hold and ran off, yelping. Daniel headed for the dining room. He was hungry. He spent the day by the pool, under an umbrella, reading and doing crossword puzzles. Occasionally he went to the pool bar and ordered fruit drinks, waiting patiently for his turn as revelers kidded and flirted with each other, trading quips with the bartenders.

For the next few nights, the dream returned. On the fourth night, as Daniel hovered above the loping animal and it veered toward the mountains, Daniel stooped like a hawk, his own indistinct form blending with that of the beast. He was swept away with an exhilaration he had never felt before.

x  x  x  x  x

He sat with his parents on the patio, eating breakfast. His father pored over an article in a medical journal as he sipped his coffee. His mother, bored and fidgety when she was away from her work, glanced around the patio, and wrinkled her nose as a man three tables away lit up a cigar. She fussed with her napkin. A new flock of tourists had arrived and the buffet was busy. As Daniel was toying with his toast and jam, a waiter slipped a CD into the stereo beside the drinks cooler, and African rhythms and guitars filled the air. Same table, Daniel mused, same food, same boring tunes.

"Daniel, what on earth has happened to your hands?"

He looked down. Grime discolored his skin. Dirt was caked under cracked fingernails.

"Not what you'd call pianist's delicate digits," his father commented, looking up from his journal. His hands, Daniel often thought, were the only part of his body with any strength. A lifetime of piano playing had hardened muscles and tendons. He kept his nails manicured, his skin, except his fingertips where they touched the keys, soft. A pianist, every music teacher he had ever had reminded him, must look after his hands. But now he was as mystified as his mother.

"Well?" she said.

"Um," he began, wishing that he was a better liar. He knew an I-don't-know wouldn't satisfy his parents. "I fell on the way to breakfast," he said. "There's this ratty little dog, I think it belongs to the maid, and it chases me every morning. And I fell."

His mother pushed a few strands of hair from her damp forehead. The day was already heating up. "Well, be more careful," she advised, just as a waitress came to the table to remove the plates.

Daniel relaxed. The waitress bent across the table for his plate. Her shirt fell away from her body, revealing the tops of her breasts and a white bra. Daniel diverted his gaze, conscious of her warmth, the odors of her body. He breathed deeply. She straightened up and moved away from the table.

× × × × ×

The powerful creature ran, climbing a steep stony slope to a plateau. The night sky, obscured by clouds, gave no light, but the beast saw easily enough as it sprinted across the dry ground, skirting the small villages, sniffing wood smoke, burned lamp oil, humans, pigs, chickens, horses. In the fields around the tiny settlements, the sharp, heavy odor of goat, the thick scent of cow. Tongue lolling, the beast paced itself, running for the sheer joy of movement, rejoicing in its power and agility, ears tuned to the myriad sounds of the night, eyes afire. When thirsty, it lapped mountain spring water from rocky pools; when hunger pangs creased its stomach, it knew where to find succulent flesh and marrow, and rich, hot blood.

× × × × ×

Daniel languished on a chaise lounge in the shade of a tree on the beach, watching the waves break on the coral fifty yards from shore. A warm breeze from the water carried the scent of salt and fish. Piano practice had begun to bore him. He no longer read his books or worked on his puzzles; he preferred to soak up the heat and watch and listen. He heard snatches of conversation whenever he wished, even at a distance. He drew odors from the air at will—the coconut-scented sunblock that the woman walking the shore in front of him had rubbed on her body; beer and rum from the bar; and a hundred different sweats.

He had begun to take some sun, and already a light, golden tan tinged his skin. And he no longer felt ashamed to walk barechested along the beach. Though his body was slender and undeveloped compared to the hard muscular Cuban men, he glowed with the new power in his limbs.

His body seemed to burst with energy. He felt as if he could run for miles, swim across the Caribbean. The changes had frightened Daniel at first, but now he accepted—welcomed—them without question. The strange occurrences, like the lunchtime he found himself sitting down to a plate of bloodrare roast beef smothered in rich gravy, the breakfast when he tipped his plate to his lips and sucked bacon fat into his mouth, even the morning he rose from the toilet seat and noticed, to his amazement, shreds of fur in his stools—none of these things troubled him. Something was happening to him. And he wanted it more than he had ever desired anything.

x x x x x

"Cheers," said his father.

Daniel and his parents clinked glasses. He was allowed wine with dinner that evening, to celebrate. His father had received an award at the conference, and one of his papers was to be published in a medical journal out of Havana.

"It's not exactly *Lancet*," his mother had said when she announced the news, "but it's an honor nevertheless."

They made small talk for a while. Daniel's father commented on Daniel's change in eating habits, apparently pleased. "From vegan to voracious," he said. Daniel didn't tell them he had no need for his puffers any more, or that his medications lay in the bottom of the wastebasket in his room. His mother would worry. His parents soon fell into shoptalk. Daniel got up from his chair and made his way to the long buffet table, picking up a new plate. He selected a broiled fish, which had been cooked head and all, and a thick slice of ham.

As he turned away, he noticed a young woman serving fresh fruit behind a table in the corner. Her black skin contrasted sharply with her crisp white smock. As she moved, placing oozing slices of papaya on a platter with a spatula, the supple muscles in her forearms flexed; her long fingers seemed to caress the fruit. Daniel sucked in the rich scents—pineapple, mango, banana, and the thick cream in the bowl at the end of the table; the woman's hair, the perfume that floated like a cloud above the layer of perspiration. She had wide eyes, slightly slanted, and thick, wiry hair drawn back from her face and held behind her head with a simple copper ring that glowed when she moved her head.

Daniel returned to his table. He cut his ham into thick slices and pushed them into his mouth, gulping them down, his eyes directed across the room to the woman behind the fruit stand.

"What are you staring at?" his mother demanded.

"I think it's that girl serving the fruit," his father suggested, pointing with his chin.

His parents looked in the direction indicated. At that moment, Daniel cut the head off his fish and popped it into his mouth, chomping noisily. Neither parent noticed.

"Daniel, you really must stop this ogling," his mother said. "It's rude and demeaning. You, above all people, should know women aren't objects. You were raised better."

Behind his mother's head, Daniel saw the woman look his way. She fixed him with her eyes, her face expressionless. She knows, he thought.

x x x x x

Later, lying in bed, Daniel easily directed his hearing to the next room, where his parents went through their preparation for bed.

"Did you notice your son at dinner? You need to talk to him about his staring. He's stripping them naked with his eyes. It's embarrassing."

"Oh, leave him alone. He's finally—at his age! —showing an interest in females and you're upset about it. Well, I'm not. Frankly, I was beginning to wonder about him."

"Oh, for heaven's sake! Just because he hasn't fallen for the whole do-it-if-it-feels-good ethic these days. I don't want him to become a boor."

x x x x x

Daniel awakened early with the familiar comfortable ache and languor in his limbs. Standing at the sink, he scrubbed his hands with a brush, scouring the dirt from beneath his nails and the creases in the skin around his knuckles. He showered and brushed his teeth, barely noting that one of his front teeth was chipped, combed his hair, removing a burr, and put on a pair of shorts and a tight T-shirt.

He listened outside his parents' room, heard his father's snore and his mother's deep breathing, and headed to breakfast without them. The little terrier cowered under its couch, whining, ears flat to its head, shivering as he passed.

In the dining room, Daniel asked the man making the omelets for three raw eggs. The man shrugged, cracked the eggs into a cup, and put it on Daniel's tray. Daniel selected a half dozen pork sausages, spooning grease onto his plate, and took a piece of toast. Alone at his table, he poured the eggs down his throat, washing them down with hot black coffee, then made a sandwich of sausages slathered with ketchup and melted fat.

Afterwards, he strolled into the lobby shop and bought a bathing suit. In his room, he donned the new trunks, oiled his body with sunblock, and headed for the beach. He took a swim, reapplied sunblock, and walked the length of the beach, gathering snatches of conversation and eddies of smells, squeezing wet sand between his toes, reveling in the hot caress of sun on his skin. He turned and retraced his steps to the beach bar. He ordered a beer and stood sipping it, watching the volleyball game.

She was there, among eight shouting and laughing players, a mix of tourists and hotel staff. One of the tourists, a heavy, well-built man in his twenties, crowed whenever his team scored a point. At length, a Cuban dropped out, picking up a tank top from a chair nearby and heading toward the main building. The game ceased. Heads swiveled.

"What about him?" someone said. Eyes focused on Daniel.

"Why not?" the muscular guy jeered, addressing the short-handed team. "It's not like you'll catch up to us anyway. Not with him on your team."

Daniel stared at the man. "I'll play," he said.

The game continued. Daniel knew the rules, knew how to play from lessons at school, classes he had attended only under duress. To his surprise, he held his own, fumbling a few balls at first, then improving rapidly. What he lacked in experience he made up for with speed and agility. Soon he was at the net, and his team had caught up. He watched intently as the young woman from the dining room fruit stand prepared to serve. She wore a banana yellow bikini. Daniel took in her smells, noted the muscles rippling beneath the skin of her thighs, the sheen of sweat across the tops of her breasts. She served overhand. Behind him, his teammates set up the ball. Daniel jumped, timing his spike perfectly. His hand was far above the net when he drove the ball downward. It slammed—thwack!—into the chest of the man who had mocked him earlier. His arms windmilling, the man stumbled backwards and sat down heavily, grunting. Cheers from behind Daniel. The man shook his head, fixed Daniel with a murderous look as his face turned crimson. He leaped to his feet and rushed across the sand, ducking under the net.

"I'll teach you to—"

Daniel sidestepped the rush and spun the man around, tripping him. As the man crashed to the sand, Daniel dropped one knee to the man's chest and gripped his throat with one hand. He snarled, baring his teeth, squeezing his fingers tighter, his tendons contracting like piano wire, oblivious to the choking and splutters coming from the man's open mouth.

"Let him go!" someone yelled.

"He's choking him," came another voice from behind Daniel. Arms pulled him backwards. He looked up. She was watching him, wide-eyed, her mouth open, a string of spittle joining her lips. She licked it away, closed her mouth, the intimation of a smile crossing her lips.

Daniel allowed himself to be pulled to his feet. He brushed sand from his knees, then walked away. That afternoon, he sat at his keyboard, earphones clamped to his head so that only he could hear. He played by ear, music he normally refused even to acknowledge. He surrendered to the passion of Liszt, alternately pounding and caressing the keys. After a while, he played impromptu, creating as he went, his torso rising and dipping, his head bobbing, sweat dripping from his brow. He played and played, insanely, with no control but that imposed by the music, until he fell from his chair from exhaustion.

✗ ✗ ✗ ✗ ✗

The beach party, to be held on Daniel's last night in Cuba, had been the talk of the resort for a week. Daniel had joined his parents in their derision, pretending all the while. The hypnotic rhythm of drums could be heard as the three family members strolled through the grounds to their rooms after dinner. Daniel waited, fidgeting, drumming his fingers, until he heard the deep breathing of sleep through the wall, then dressed and left his room.

Tables and chairs had been set up in the sand. A bonfire crackled, and the bar was crowded and raucous. A large number of resort guests had turned up, along with a few workers. Daniel joined the crush at the bar, his eyes scanning the beach. He drank off his first beer quickly and ordered another, carrying it to the edge of the water. He stood ankle deep in the lapping waves, facing the shore. Finally he caught sight of her. She was dancing with one of the young men who regularly played beach volleyball.

The tune ended and another began, with a faster beat that seemed to reach out and clutch him at the center. The young woman left her partner and approached Daniel. She wore a white dress with full skirt and a scoop neck. She was barefoot, and copper bracelets adorned her wrists. She took Daniel's hand and led him to the patch of sand where the dancing was taking place. They said nothing to one another. Daniel watched her feet, immediately picked up the simple steps and gave himself up to the sounds.

The surf pounded, an arrhythmic backdrop for the narcotic complex cadence of the drums. The music seeped down into him, slaking a need in him, the way spring water is absorbed by dry, porous rock. The woman moved with the grace of a cat, the intensity of a storm. The drum beats welded the two of them together as their arms moved, their feet pounded the sand, their eyes tenaciously set on each other.

Daniel heard only the surf and the drums and her breathing, felt only her heat.

✕ ✕ ✕ ✕ ✕

The dance had ended late, and the full moon was rising. Daniel paced his room, unable, despite his fatigue, to stop moving. He stripped off his damp clothing, took a shower, dressed in dry trousers and T-shirt. On his dresser top, his suitcases sat open. In one, clothes and shoes in a jumble; in the other, a chaos of CDs, DVDs, books, and sheet music. Departure time was seven a.m.

He heard something outside. He shut off the air conditioner, slid open the patio door. A gecko scurried across the stones. Daniel was keenly aware of crickets, insects moving in the grass, the soft clatter of palmetto fronds in the night breeze. And something else. The quiet footfalls of an animal, padding restlessly back and forth behind the resort. A soft growl.

Daniel felt his heart accelerate, his breathing become shallow and rapid. He backed into his room, then strode to the patio, returned to the room, took a glass of water in the bathroom, stalked to the patio door once more. He directed his attention to his parents' room, the sounds of their sleeping. He glanced at his computer, his keyboard, his books, the airplane ticket at the edge of his desk. He heard another growl, more distant this time, then sensed rather than heard the footfalls recede.

Daniel looked into his room once more, then stepped across the threshold. The waving palmetto fronds scattered splinters of moonlight across the patio. Daniel made for the beach. He strode past the empty bar, the tables and upended chairs, far down the strand, where waves crashing against the reef hurled streaks of spume into the air. Piece by piece, he flung his clothing away until he was naked. He lay down on the damp sand, waiting for sleep.


*Author's note:*

In Greek mythology, the god Apollo is associated with music, poetry, harmony, and reason. We find his spirit also in mathematics and classical architecture. He favours reason and balance. Dionysos is sometimes referred to as "the party god," but that's too simplistic. He represents the passions, energy, creativity, and sexuality. If Apollo is classical, Dionysos is with the Romantics. It is sometimes said that the human personality contains both gods, and we are happiest when there is a balance between their spirits.

# X X X X X

*William Bell was born in Toronto in 1945. He has been a high school English teacher and department head, and an instructor at the Harbin University of Science and Technology, the Foreign Affairs College (both in China), and the University of British Columbia. He has won the Belgium Prize for Excellence, the Ruth Schwartz Award, the Mr. Christie's Book Award, and the Canadian Library Association's Young Adult Book Award. Bell's books include* Crabbe, Absolutely Invincible, Five Days of the Ghost, Forbidden City, No Signature, Speak to the Earth, Zack, Stones, Alma, *and* Just Some Stuff I Wrote.

# The Collapse

## Kathy Stinson

The digital clock on the dash of my dad's car said barely past four, but dark clouds hung so heavily over the roadway I had to switch on the headlights. I hadn't been back to our old neighborhood since we'd moved away a couple of years ago, when my mom landed a job with the government. I'd thought when I first set out that I might drive by my old house, but as dusk fell early with the threat of rain, I decided to just get to Kohl's as soon as I could. No point driving in a storm if I could avoid it.

The Asher house was a sprawling multi-level just north of town, way larger than ours in town had been, but Kohl's parents had money, lots of it, and a house that said so. It was an odd mix of modern and traditional styles, people said, designed by his mother, some modern equivalent of Picasso or something and also a big name architect. One section, the tallest, was old limestone. Three single-story wings at the back were simple stucco. A covered veranda ran across the front. What I'd always thought the coolest feature of the house was the octagonal turret at one corner. That and the pool out front. With slabs of granite instead of tile all around it, and a dark grey liner instead of standard turquoise, it was like a deep, dark, natural grotto. I'd heard a lot of people swam in it naked at parties—after I'd moved away.

When I was little, my grandmother often said things like, "Now, there's a house with a cheerful face," or "Look at that house, John, doesn't it look surprised?" I'd never really got what she meant, till I turned up Kohl's long driveway. Especially in the way it was reflected in the still, black pool out front, the house and the skeletal trees around it seemed . . . melancholy. I can't think of any other word to describe it. I almost wished I hadn't come.

I hadn't seen Kohl's face at any window; he hadn't yet opened the door to say, "Hi John, come on in." So it wasn't too late to turn around and leave. But even though we'd lost touch when my family moved away, we had been friends, and now Kohl was very sick. When he'd called last night, asking me to please come, he sounded pretty nervous. Of dying? Dying alone? Or of the possibility I might say no? He'd made it sound on the phone as if I were his best friend. Which was odd. Even when I used to come over regularly, to watch movies, play games on his computer, or fool around on his guitar, I never felt I really knew him all that well.

Except for living in such an amazing house—I'd scored a lot of points with girls for being friends with the guy who lived here—he'd sure had his share of rotten luck. I heard last April that both his parents were killed in a car crash during some freak blizzard. It made the news because of his father being a famous ex-rock star. Friends with Alice Cooper, Ozzy Osbourne, the whole bit. Now Kohl was sick. I couldn't leave. As I took in the reflection of those sorry windows, the drooping line of the eaves, and the pointed roof of the turret, I couldn't help thinking—no, it was more of a *feeling*, an ominous, "this may be the end of an era" kind of thing.

Quickly I grabbed my duffel bag from the trunk—it would just be a few days—and started up the slope of lawn toward the house. One step leading to the veranda, I noticed, was broken; the paint on the window frames was flaking. Could the house have deteriorated this much since April? I didn't think Kohl's parents would have let things go like this. In the corner of the veranda sat a glass table and several chairs heaped with brown, curling leaves. Kohl and a bunch of guys had shared more than a few beers there, but you couldn't imagine sitting outside on a raw day like the day I arrived.

Before I knocked on the door, it opened. A guy about my age, late high school, came out holding a small suitcase. Already hurrying down the steps, he said, "He's in his studio."

"His what?"

"Used to be his father's music room," he called back to me from the driveway. "He's all yours now. Good luck."

The door stood open, so I went in. Things in the arched hallway leading to one of the back wings were familiar, but changed somehow since I'd last seen them. Paintings I'd liked or been indifferent to looked ugly. Several portraits in the style of Picasso had an almost sinister attitude about them. Carpets were dingier than I remembered. In one room I passed, cushions were strewn around the floor, along with empty bottles, glasses, and several not-empty ashtrays. The evidence of party added strangely to the feeling of despair that hung over everything.

The music room, now Kohl's studio, was no better. The only light came from a single lamp. Books and papers were heaped on chairs and tables, and an oily paint palette lay on one. A few smeary canvasses leaned against dusty bookshelves. I didn't see Kohl stretched out on a couch in the corner of the dim room till I went to open one of the window blinds and he snapped at me. "Don't!"

"Nice way to welcome an old friend. How are ya?"

"Sorry," he said, getting up. "Some days my eyes just can't take the light." Kohl had always been a bit funny looking, with big ears, a high forehead, and somewhat bulging eyes, but now those eyes were too bright, his skin too pale. His hair, down to his shoulders—he'd never worn it long before—was almost white; wispy like the cobweb stuff people use to decorate haunted houses at Hallowe'en.

Kohl slapped me on the back. "Thanks for coming."

"No problem."

He started babbling then in an almost frenzied way. Something about "faces in the mirror" and "grey paragraphs." That couldn't be what he actually said, and I couldn't tell if he was talking about a painting, a book he was reading, or what. Suddenly he stopped, leaned against the back of a chair and started humming a tune I didn't recognize. Had he been drinking? Was he high? Both?

When he started talking again, it was at a speed resembling normal, but now he sounded like an actor pouring out an anguished soliloquy on stage. He was going on about some kind of "sensory disorder" that supposedly ran in his family. His mother'd had it—I never knew—and his grandfather. "Too much light hurts my eyes," he said. "Music is an attack on my ears, my whole head. But sometimes I can enjoy a little guitar. I can't stand anything even slightly rough against my skin. And my stomach can tolerate only really bland food."

"No more ordering from Pizza Pizzazz for you, I guess, eh?"

He looked at me as if trying to figure out what language I was speaking, then laughed. No, he didn't laugh; he giggled. I'd forgotten how he sometimes used to do that. "I knew asking you to come was the right thing to do," he said. "You're going to be good for me, John." He sent me to the wine cellar for a bottle of Merlot.

The room we raided as thirteen-year-olds once when his parents were away was cold, damp, and very small. I grabbed two bottles from the wall-sized rack and went back upstairs as fast as I could. Kohl had glasses ready, and shaking hands.

Pouring us each some wine, I said, "Is there any treatment for this thing you've got?"

"You'll cheer me up." Barely pausing to take a breath, but as if a switch had clicked in his brain, he said, "Everything scares me. Everything about now, and everything about what might happen some day. Everything." He started pacing the room.

"Are you scared of me?" I asked, thinking I was being funny and that maybe this kind of kidding around was what Kohl wanted from me.

"I'd stop being scared if I knew how. I would, you know. If I knew."

"Remember what our old swim coach used to say: You have nothing to fear but fear itself."

"Beatty may have thought fear was nothing—" Kohl giggled a shrill titter. "But I'm afraid it's going to do me in!"

Maybe Kohl did have some kind of sensory disorder, but there had to be something mental going on with him too. Possibly because of too much dope, or maybe he was into harder stuff now. But I couldn't help thinking it might have something to do with the house, too. "Hey, Kohl, how about I get you away from here for a while? We could go for a drive. It'll be dark out now—no light to bother your eyes?"

"I can't," he said. "My sister . . . is very sick."

I'd forgotten his sister. A quiet girl, odder even than her brother. "Has she got the thing you have?"

He shook his head. "Allergies. At first they were just to normal things like cats and house dust." He spoke in the same agitated way he had earlier, but not as disjointedly, or so it seemed. Maybe with a couple of glasses of wine in me, it was just easier for me to make sense of him. "Things like shampoo and paper started bothering her," he went on, "and then she developed food allergies. More and more all the time. Now practically everything gives her hives or asthma or makes her . . ." he giggled " . . . puke."

"Has she seen a doctor?"

"Doctors don't know anything." Kohl hurried to a desk under the window, opened a drawer, and closed it again. "They can't explain the other thing that happens either."

"Which is . . .?"

"Every so often, she passes out. Sometimes for a few minutes, sometimes for longer. It might be because of the allergies, but it seems like something else. She goes totally stiff when it happens. Totally."

"I can see why you don't want to leave her."

Just then, Miranda, in a long white nightgown, passed along the hallway outside Kohl's studio. I shivered. I looked at Kohl to see if he'd noticed her effect on me, but his pale face was buried in his hands; he was crying.

"Is there anything I can do for her?" I realized that at another time, in another place, my question could be taken any number of lewd ways. But in that house, it was like there was no other time or place.

"No. She's gone to bed." There was something horribly final-sounding about how he said it.

I'd taken about as much as I could of our reunion for one day. Before I'd got here I'd been hungry, but now, even though I hadn't eaten, I had no appetite at all. "Maybe I'll hit the sack, too, then."

Kohl led me back through the arched hallway, past the wing where I remembered Miranda's room was, and across the front hall. He was leading me to the turret. I was glad of that, until he pushed open the door.

Everything about my room gave off the same sorry funk that hung over the rest of the house.

After he left me, I remembered I was supposed to call my parents to tell them I'd arrived. I dug my phone out of the pocket of my bag. *No Service* said the display. I forced myself to make the effort to leave my room to find a phone. I found one in the kitchen. There was such a crackle on the line I could hardly make myself heard, but I managed to get across that I was here, and yes, I'd be home in time for Thanksgiving dinner on Monday.

The next day I suggested we play computer games or watch a movie, thinking some of our old-time activities might help cheer Kohl up, but his computer had crashed, he said, and of course he couldn't look at movies; the colours were too bright, the soundtracks too loud. He suggested I join him in his studio, and I went along. My attempts with a paintbrush were pathetic; he didn't care.

He hadn't done more than a few bloody red strokes before he stopped and asked me to read to him. I was surprised to find I didn't mind reading aloud, even if Kohl's taste in books was a bit weird. I mean, who reads Edgar Allan Poe any more?

After that, we shared a joint and he fooled around on his guitar, coming up with wild lyrics to go with sounds I guess he thought were musical. As he jumped from one thing to the next with a kind of hyper energy, I kept getting the sense he was walking some really fine wire he could go hurtling off at any time.

By late afternoon, I'd had it with pretending I could paint; with trying to make jokes that either fell flat or got laughed at in that hysterical giggle of Kohl's that I thought would drive me nuts; with his endless rants about how things like the lichens growing on the roof have feelings, and so does the roof. I'd had it with trying to be Mister Golden Sun in the face of the glumness that poured out of my friend and the very walls of his bleak house, that seemed somehow to be slowly closing in on us.

Kohl was in the middle of showing me some book about an old church somewhere, when I knew suddenly that I couldn't spend another day, or night, in his house. I had to leave. If he needed company, he'd have to call somebody else. I was about to tell him so, when Miranda appeared, in the same nightgown I'd seen her in the previous night.

"Want some?" She held out a bag of something white. "Purely medicinal, of course, but you'll like it."

I did. I think Kohl did too, but it's hard to remember everything.

When he next appeared—I think it was the next day—he seemed, unlike me, full of a restless energy. He picked up a book and after a few minutes set it down. He splashed muddy paint on a canvas, then flitted to his guitar, which he tuned, and set aside. He muttered words I couldn't be bothered trying to make sense of any more. Then he said, "Her medicine. She needs medicine." He dashed off, leaving me alone.

I thought of going, then, without telling him. But the lethargy that had been creeping into me since I'd got here had become so heavy I couldn't move. Of course, as soon as Kohl came back from tending to Miranda, I knew I should have.

Sweat beaded on his forehead. He was breathing fast. "She's dead," he said.

A chill crawled over my body, like newly hatched spiders.

"She must have OD'd. You have to help me, John." His eyes were round with terror, but his words came out hoarsely, as much a threat as a plea.

"Of course." I returned to the wine cellar and brought up a case so I wouldn't have to go back down again soon. Collecting myself, knowing I had to help my old friend if I could, I said, "Who should I call? What funeral home?"

He ground the heels of his hands into his eyes.

"Do you remember who you used when your parents . . . ?"

"We have to get her to the basement."

"What are you talking about? We've got to call. . . ." A doctor? Too late for that. The police? Would they think we'd done something wrong? Had we? A funeral home. Like I'd said before. In spite of knowing I had to keep my wits about me, I gulped down a glassful of unfamiliar smoky red wine and poured another.

Kohl wailed, "If someone comes, they'll take her!" He tore at his hair, pounded his thighs with his fists. Snot ran out his nose, and when he tried to wipe it away, it stuck to the back of his hand and got caught in his hair. He cried, "You've got to help me get her down to the basement!"

"Okay," I said. "Okay. At least, we won't call, not right away."

I'd have to sober up before we could call anyone. I couldn't believe how one glass of wine—or was it two?—could have hit me so hard. "But Kohl, we can't keep her here. When people die . . ." there was only one way to say it ". . . they rot."

"That's why you have to help me. Right now! You have to!"

"Kohl, you didn't . . . do something . . . did you? To your sister?"

Why had I come here? Why hadn't I left with that guy who was leaving when I got here?

"We're twi-i-i-ins!" It was like the word was being ripped out of him along with his tongue. He wiped his snotty hands on his shirt. "Remember that? We're twins; she's all I've got, John! Just her and this godforsaken house!" His shoulders shook with his sobbing.

I knocked back another glass of wine so I wouldn't have to think about how bizarre it was, what Kohl wanted. Then, half convincing myself that laying Miranda out on one of the big sofas in the media room till we called the funeral people wasn't such a bad idea, I followed Kohl as he carried her to the basement.

Kathy Stinson                                                      73

Into its gloom he took her, cradled stiffly in his arms, a pale tie-dyed scarf draped discreetly over her face. And I followed, even when he turned toward the part of the basement I knew was under the turret. I'd heard rumors about things Kohl's parents and their friends did in there at parties, but I'd never been in it. Kohl said, "There's a place down here where no one will find her."

It made as much sense as anything I'd heard him say since I'd got here. In other words, it was craziness. While Kohl tugged on a heavy iron door, he made me hold Miranda. Rigor mortis was already setting in and she weighed almost nothing. As he forced the door open, it grated on its hinges. Beyond the doorway was total darkness. Why was I here?

When Kohl flicked the light switch, nothing happened. "Must be burnt out," he whispered.

Because he had whispered, I did too. "What's this room for, anyhow?"

"Something to do with a dungeon game my dad used to play with guests."

I was sorry I'd asked.

A sudden rasping sound made me jump. The room was flooded with light. It seemed so at first, anyway, but once the flare of the match settled and Kohl got a candle lit, there was just enough light to see spiders scurrying away in the dampness seeping down the concrete walls. And . . . oh, God. . . .

. . . an open coffin, with the lid pushed back.

"Kohl, we can't," I said, but whatever was in that wine, or last night's pot, left me with no conviction about anything.

"Put her in," he said.

And I did. The scarf fell from her face.

Miranda's resemblance to her brother was remarkable—thin lips, high forehead, wispy hair. But the deep hollows under Kohl's eyes made him look almost more dead than his sister.

Across Miranda's cheeks was a sort of blush, as if she—or he—had applied make-up. Kohl stared at her for a long time, his lips trembling.

I might have just stood there the rest of my life, but when Kohl closed the lid of the coffin and handed me a screwdriver, I helped him screw it down. He blew out the candle and dragged shut the iron door. I winced at the grating sound it made against the concrete floor.

"How's that on *your* ears?" I asked on the way back upstairs, wanting to get his mind, and mine, on something other than what we had just done.

"Hurts," he whined. I could see from how he grimaced that it did.

We had another drink together, not talking. The wine was potent and good. I wondered if there was more to it than just fermented grapes, but didn't wonder about it a lot.

Kohl's face was as pale as I'd ever seen it, and his eyes. . . . People sometimes say, "The lights are on but nobody's home," but in Kohl's case, the lights weren't even on. He spent the next few hours, or maybe it was only a few minutes, just sitting, staring at nothing. If I left the room, he followed me, and sat and stared some more. I kept thinking he wanted to tell me something, something I probably wouldn't want to know, but when he did speak, all he said, in his quivery little voice, was, "If you leave me, John, I'll . . . I'll fall apart." I think by then I was as terrified as he was.

I might have fallen asleep for a while though; I wasn't sure. When I next saw Kohl, his shirt and jeans were rumpled, as if he'd slept in them, but not well.

Time somehow got lost in the aimless hours that passed in that gloomy house, made gloomier by what seeped up to us from the basement. That night, or it could have been a week later—I didn't know or care—I tried to sleep. I'd had enough to drink, I should have just passed out, but no matter how I arranged my pillows or tried counting backwards from a thousand by sixes, I was as restless as the wind that blew outside my window. I'm not normally nervous of storms—did I really know what "normal" was any more? I doubt it—but that night, with every gust, my heart beat more quickly. In the pauses between them, I held my breath, waiting for the next.

During one pause, as I waited for the wind to lash against the panes, I thought I heard a sound. Something in the house. Moving. I didn't think it was Kohl. He hadn't bothered to move, even to follow me around, in—I couldn't say for how long. He just sat and stared at nothing. Whatever it was I'd heard, after the wind again rose and died, the house was silent.

Finally I started to drift off, when I heard a low, dull sound. I threw myself out of bed—I would never sleep!—and accidentally sent an empty wine bottle rolling. I grabbed my pants from the chair. This whole situation was ridiculous. I didn't have to be here. I had a perfectly good home only a few hours away. My being here wasn't doing Kohl a bit of good. I would write a quick note saying I was sorry—no, why should I apologize?—and. . . .

A light step outside my room. I stopped, my arm half into my sleeve.

A light tapping on the door. Answer it? Or pretend to be asleep? I couldn't bear the thought of facing Kohl again.

"Power's out," he said, coming in with a flashlight and closing the door behind him. He looked so haggard I knew it was just an excuse; he was terrified of being alone and it was taking all the energy he had in him to keep from going totally hysterical. "Have you heard it?" he said, breathing heavily. He rushed across the room, yanked hard on the cord to open the blinds. He pushed open the window to the full fury of the storm.

It was terrible. Clouds so dense that if there was a moon or stars that night, we couldn't see them. Wind pulling and pushing at trees, changing direction with every gust. But it was gorgeous too. An unnatural kind of light made the undersides of the clouds glow, and it shone golden on the tree branches and the uneven waters of the black pool below us. It seemed the pool was breathing, and its breath hung heavy all around the house. Around us.

"Come away from there," I said. "The cold air's not good for you." I closed the window and led Kohl gently but forcefully to a seat. "Why don't I read to you?" I grabbed an old book from a stack that had been on the dresser since the day I arrived.

I could tell as soon as I started that it was a lousy story, but Kohl sat listening intently, so I kept reading, trying hard to keep the flashlight steady.

"'Ed raised his axe and smashed it through the door. With the axe and his bare hands, he ripped at the jagged hole, not caring about the rain that pelted his shoulders or the fragments of wood that jabbed his skin. The cracking of the wood as he yanked the door apart could be heard throughout the forest.'"

By an amazing coincidence, from far away, came the indistinct but definite sound of wood cracking. It wasn't totally surprising, given the force of the storm outside, but the timing of it . . . I continued reading.

"'Ed was surprised to see, when he stepped through the broken door, a dog—large and black, with golden eyes and hot breath. The dog growled, bared its vicious teeth, and lunged. Ed brought his axe down with a thud upon its skull. The animal let out a prolonged and frightful shriek.'"

From far off, but definitely from somewhere inside the house this time, came a stifled echo of a harsh, drawn-out shriek. A coincidence? Twice? It couldn't be.

Suddenly, I saw clearly what I should have realized sooner, and would have, if I hadn't somehow lost all my perspective on things. I was the victim of a prank. Kohl had cooked it up, and the guy I'd met at the door the day I'd come—he hadn't left at all. I had no idea as to the reason for such an elaborate hoax, but maybe when you're as nuts as Kohl, reason doesn't come into anything. In any case, if the purpose of their game was to frighten me, it had worked.

Certain I'd see some sign that Kohl was acting out another part in the joke, I shone the light on him. His lips were trembling, his eyes were open wide. He was rocking from side to side. It was as good a job of "scared shitless" as you'd see on the stage of any theater.

Deciding to play my part, I placed my hand on Kohl's shoulder, as if to calm him. He continued to rock, his eyes fixed on the door of my room, his whole face rigid, it seemed, with fear. He spoke in gibberish, as if to himself. Less confident than I had been a moment earlier, that I was the butt of some joke—Kohl couldn't act *this* well—I leaned closer to hear what he was saying.

"I heard it have you heard it now? I have for minutes, hours, I dared not speak of it, for days I've heard it."

"Heard what?"

"She was alive," he mumbled, "you put her in her tomb alive, such feeble little movements I heard but dared not mention."

"She. . . ." My blood was like ice in my veins. Kohl had told me the day I arrived that his hearing was hyper-sensitive. If what he was telling me now. . . .

My knees buckled. I sank to the side of my bed. How could Miranda have been dead? What must Kohl have been hearing in all the hours before tonight? Did he hear his sister banging on the lid of her coffin? Or scratching? Calling out?

I shouted, "Why didn't you tell me?" I rose, grabbed Kohl by the shoulders, and shook him. "We could have done something! Why didn't you say something?!"

"I didn't dare I don't know how she . . . I was so sure?" His gibberish grew more and more panicked, and suddenly stopped.

To listen. I could see that he was listening. I listened, too, but heard nothing.

"She's out." Kohl's voice was high and weak. "She's coming! Shh!" He sat very still and in a moment whispered, "Did you hear that?"

I shook my head.

"Her footsteps." He jumped up then, and grabbed an empty bottle from the top of my dresser. Still facing the door he shouted, "Help me! She's here!"

The door opened. And there she stood. Thinner even, it seemed, than the night I saw her passing by Kohl's studio. With blood on her upraised hands, running in rivulets down her arms, and into the sleeves of her nightgown.

"You tried. . . " Her voice was hoarse. ". . . to kill me." A voice of the dead. With her bloodied hands, Miranda came at Kohl's neck.

The storm was howling, or it might have been me, as I careened through the arched hallway to the door and slithered like madness itself across the sodden grass. A wild light shot down the driveway ahead of me. I turned to see that the power had come back on in the house. So little light there'd been when I was inside, but now light flooded from every window. I searched the turret for a human silhouette—or two—but before I found it, a rumbling shook the earth.

I thought the storm was opening up even more dementedly than before, until I saw—I was sure—the walls of the house crumbling.

Stone by stone they fell, along with the broken stucco of the wings, and tumbled into the pool beside me. Its waters—I would never have believed it if I hadn't seen it for myself— closed with a fantastic *swoosh* over all of it, as if the Asher house, and Kohl and Miranda too, had never been.

*With apologies to Edgar Allan Poe*

# X X X X X

*Many of Kathy Stinson's more than twenty titles for toddlers, teens, and in-betweens have been published both in Canada and abroad. Several have been nominated for various readers' choice awards. Before becoming a writer, Kathy worked as a mail sorter, a waitress, and a teacher. She has enjoyed meeting readers all across Canada, and in England where she took part in an international exchange of children's authors in 1987. Born in Toronto in 1952, she received a Bicentennial Civic Award of Merit from the City of Scarborough in 1996. Kathy currently lives and writes full-time in a small hamlet near Guelph, Ontario.*

# Fever on Nipple Mountain

## Jamie Bastedo

*Interim Coroner's Report*

*The deceased, Ryan J. Bardo, is a 17-year-old cau-
casian male with no prior medical history of signifi-
cance. He was a non-smoker, needed no prescription
medications, and did not use illicit drugs or alcohol.
He was last seen by his mother, Gillian Hines, on the
morning of December 31st, leaving his Fairbanks
home at 55 Goldstream Drive by snowmobile for
what he described as "a quick spin." Journal entries
by the deceased suggest he died seven days later. His
frozen body was recovered January 12th near the
Nipple Mountain fire lookout station, located in the
Yukon River State Forest approximately 75 miles
northwest of Fairbanks.*

*The deceased was a top athlete, excelled academ-
ically and displayed an aptitude for language arts and
creative writing. He was a keen observer of nature,*

demonstrated competence in northern bush skills, and tackled mechanical problems with apparent ease. His parents and teachers report that he occasionally exhibited rapid mood swings and sporadic depression, particularly during winter, suggesting he may have suffered periodically from Seasonal Affective Disorder or SAD, otherwise known as "winter malaise."

The victim's undisclosed solo adventure to the remote Nipple Mountain fire station clearly placed him in a life-threatening wilderness predicament. However he was well equipped with the physical stamina, personal skills, and material resources required for long-term survival in this particular situation.

The exact manner of Ryan Bardo's death remains unsolved. As a contribution to the ongoing investigation of this case by the Alaska State Troopers, this Interim Coroner's Report provides all relevant details from his journal and supporting documentation that may shed light on the puzzling circumstances of his death.

*New Year's Eve*

There's nothing else to do up here so I might as well write my memoirs until Kelly sends help. A good way to beat cabin fever. I found an empty forestry fieldbook when I ransacked the cupboards looking for food. Maybe I can get it published someday. I can see it now: "A Night on Nipple Mountain." What a laugh! That should get some attention.

I found some food all right. White rice, flour, tea, and skim milk powder. Yum. It's good Dad stuffed all those power bars and moose jerky in the pack. The cook stove is toast anyway.

I guess I overdid it. I figured seventy miles was nothing for a snowmobile built to go eighty miles an hour. Mom called my new Tiger Cat "overpowered." Dad agreed but said I could probably zoom out of anything if I got into trouble—the deepest snow, the steepest hill. Right, Dad. Anything that is, except overflow. I can't tell you how much I hate overflow. Disgusting stuff! And now it's eaten my first snowmobile. Barely out of the box. Barely broken in. I work my ass off all fall at that stinking hardware store, every free second since school started, putting up with brainless work like sorting nails and sniffing paint. And now my Christmas present to myself lies sideways, like a dead horse, way down there on the river, half buried in frozen overflow mush.

It'll probably take a stick of dynamite to move it now. I must have revved that machine to full throttle a hundred times. Man, you should have seen that slush fly! I think it froze in midair. My mighty Tiger Cat didn't budge. Not a foot. I finally kicked the bloody machine over and ran for the shore. No point in going anywhere else. I knew I was stuck out here for the night and the forest fire station was my only hope.

Thank God I grabbed Dad's survival pack on the way out the door. I didn't have a clue what was in it but at least I had the brains to throw in a map before escaping. Without that, I might as well have curled up in the snow and died right then and there beside my dearly departed snow machine.

The light was fading by the time I gave up on it. But I could see the map well enough to make out the dotted trail up the mountain. I was soaked to the knees and my feet were already aching cold. I had to find that trail before my brain went numb or I ran out of daylight. I whipped out the little compass I always carry around my neck, oriented the map, then ran north along the shore till I saw some faded orange flagging tape. Bullseye! The trail was totally socked in with snow and deadfall. Nobody'd been up there for years. I leaned forward, put my legs into overdrive and started hoofing up that hill. What a slog!

I lost the trail a couple of times but I knew that up meant safety so I crashed through the jumbled spruce like a madman. Halfway up a branch smacked me in the face and knocked my glasses into the snow. I didn't even stop to look around. It was almost pitch black anyway.

I knew I'd make it when I glimpsed the fire tower above the trees. By the time I finally bust out of the woods onto the mountain's bald crown, it was so dark the wooden tower was just a silhouette against the stars. The Atco trailer beside it was a dark hulk half swallowed by snowdrifts. "Home for the holidays!" I shouted, feeling drunk with relief and ready to drop dead with exhaustion.

One side of the trailer was totally buried in snow, probably from those wild northeast winds that blow right down the valley. Thank God the door was on the other side. It was wide open, hanging on one hinge. I squinted. What I saw made me jerk backwards, almost falling on my butt. There was light enough to see several deep gouges raked clean through the aluminum door. Nice welcome! Maybe some grizz partied here last summer. Glad they're all asleep now.

I held my breath and poked my head in. I could barely make out long curving snowdrifts covering half the floor. They were shaped just like the claw marks on the door, only ten times bigger. For a second I forgot my aching legs and wanted to run like hell back down the mountain. I slapped my frozen cheeks. "Get a grip, Ryan!" I shouted into the blackness. "It's only snow!"

I finally got the nerve to step inside. My legs were so stiff I could barely walk. My boots were cement galoshes, at least ten pounds each. Clumps of frozen slush the size of tennis balls dangled from the laces. I had to laugh out loud as I clomped around, trying to warm my feet, while the flimsy plywood floor boomed like a bloody kettledrum.

I must have been in the second stage of hypothermia. You know, when your brain starts shutting down and you're feeling quite jolly—just before you pass out. Then an odd thought struck me: get warm or die.

I was chilling out fast. All the sweat from barging up that damned hill left me cold and clammy, sucking heat from my skin with every move. I figured this beat-up old trailer must have some kind of heater. After digging blindly through Dad's survival pack, I found a flashlight and some matches. You saved me, Dad! There it was, beside a rusty old sink. A wall-mounted propane heater. Luckily I'd used one of these babies before, out at science camp last summer. One of our instructors called it "The widow-maker" but he never said why. Propane heaters can be tricky to light, especially old battle-axes like this.

I trudged back outside, found a hundred-pound propane tank, and gave it a shake. Sweet! About half full. So far so good. After going through about thirty matches I finally fired up the old girl. It sure stank of propane but boy, did it throw heat—so much, the stovepipe glowed red. The widow-maker seems to have two settings: blast furnace or stone cold.

What I did next was really stupid. My hands were okay but I didn't have a clue about my feet. Couldn't feel them at all. It was like they'd fallen off. I just couldn't wait for my boots to thaw. In some weird kind of fit I started bashing the ice balls off my laces with my one and only flashlight. Of course after a couple of good bashes the flashlight died. Duh! Trapped in the dark in my frozen boots. Nothing to see but the glowing stovepipe and cold stars out the window. I flopped around on the floor like a dying fish, groping for my pack. I found it leaning against the stove. The pack was so hot it reeked of burnt plastic. I could've burned the place down! But I found what I wanted: Dad's hunting knife. Then I hacked those boots right off my feet. Like I say—stupid!!

I don't know what got into me. I even scared myself. Mom calls it a tizzy. I call it cabin fever. It only happens in the winter. Sometimes I'll start yelling at the dog for no reason. Or get paranoid over nothing, like a door creaking or a tree branch scratching the house. I can't explain it. Mom's doctor said I should get the heck outside when I feel that way. "Give the boy some air, some sunlight," he told her. Sure. What sunlight is there this time of year?!

Anyway, I had a bad case of the fever over the holidays when it dropped to minus forty and nobody wanted to go outside. Not even Kelly, who planned our secret New Year's adventure to Nipple Mountain. He stayed indoors for ten days straight watching TV. Talk about boring! So when it warmed up to minus twenty-five, things looked pretty rosy to me. But no, Kelly chickened out at the last minute. He phoned to say his folks would ground him for the rest of the holidays if we got caught. "Safety freaks," he called them. The heck with Kelly. I'd go alone.

I was going snaky. When I got spooked by a toaster popping up, I knew I was finished. I had to escape or go bonkers. I sent Kelly a quick e-mail saying I was going anyway and would be back in town for the New Year's fireworks at midnight. I told him not to spill the beans to anyone unless I didn't show by then. Nobody would miss me. My parents would be out partying till two a.m. at least. "Just a quick spin," I told them. Then I screamed outta town on my new machine, headed straight for the famous Nipple Mountain.

As I blasted down the trail, I gulped at the cool wind rushing past me like a drowning man coming up for air. I tipped the visor of my helmet way back and drank in the feeble arctic sunshine with wide-open eyeballs. I breathed easier with each passing mile into the bush, away from the prison walls and choking air of town. God, it felt good to cut loose! I was

Wolfman shedding his fur. I imagined huge hairy clumps of it falling onto the swirling snow behind me.

Good thing Dad packed a candle. I'm writing by candle-light now. It's so dark up here. Found some signal flares too. Kelly should've opened my e-mail by now. Maybe he'll surprise me and show up for the first annual Nipple Mountain fire-works show. I'm gonna try climbing the fire tower and hail a taxi outta here.

> *This is the longest of Ryan Bardo's entries. From this point they become increasingly terse and cryptic, perhaps reflecting his growing anxiety at being trapped on the mountain.*

### New Year's Day

Wrote way too long yesterday. Eyes hurt without my glass-es. Now down to a quarter candle. Old propane lamp dangling from ceiling but its mantle is in tatters. Can't risk pouring more half-baked propane into the air. Widow-maker stinks bad enough. Head feels like it's packed full of week-old porridge. Must've been all the propane I guzzled while asleep. Well, sort of asleep. Dad's emergency blanket is like sleeping in tinfoil. It makes an irksome, crinkling noise with every breath. Maddening! And I got up about twenty times turning the heater on and off. Sweat and gag, or shiver and shake. That's how I par-tied the night away.

Took a chance and pulled the widow-maker apart. Regulator filthy so I brushed it out with a toothbrush. Dad thinks of everything. Found a vice-clamp in pack to tighten hose connection. Now at least I can control the heat. But she still stinks real bad. Must find that leak. Used up precious day-light fixing her. It's so dark, so soon. Must conserve candle just in case. But I have to write about last night while it's still fresh.

Must have been around midnight. Lost watch wrestling with snowmobile so can't say for sure. Going loony in the trailer so I stuffed my sock feet into plastic bags and climbed the fire tower. Almost wiped out on ladder. Relief to get some real air. Tear-jerking view of the wild river valley from up top. Incredible. No moon. No cabins. No roving snowmobiles. But amazingly bright. Snow almost glowing, especially on the mountain. A giant milk-white breast. Kelly would've liked that!

No wind. Nothing. So still I could hear blood pumping through my brain. Awesome! Then, a New Year's treat just for me: a volcano of northern lights erupted right over the tower. Pink, yellow, green. Cosmic! Words useless. Thought I heard them crackling but maybe hallucinating. Shouted "Happy New Year!" to the stars, then fired off a bunch of green and red flares. Got carried away but saved a few for any choppers or low flying planes. Sky watched until my feet froze.

Halfway down ladder I spotted a flash to the north. Somebody else celebrating New Year's? Climbed back up just in time to see a pale blue flare way down the valley. Reached up into sky like a big fist. Never seen a blue flare before. Slow motion. Good show. Little light below it. Also blue. Must be a cabin. How did I miss it? Might make it on foot. Must fix boots.

*January 2nd*

Friggin' cold. Wind picking up. Tried to fix boots with duct tape from Dad's pack. Look goofy but at least keeps the snow out. Managed to fix cook stove. Some animal chewed its propane hose outside. Cut hose clean, then spliced with tape. Just in time. Getting pretty thirsty. Widow-maker useless for melting snow. Door wide open in morning. Some critter stole all my moose jerky last night. No tracks. At least now I can fry up some bush buns. Even found baking powder and sugar in cupboard. Feel like Robinson Crusoe. Won't starve to death up here. Anyway it's something to do to keep my mind occupied until Kelly sends help. Why the hell hasn't he sent someone yet?

Climbed tower again last night. I like it. I can breathe. I'd sleep up there if it weren't so damned cold. Blue cabin light brighter. Who??

*January 3rd*

Made second batch of bush buns. Not bad though texture needs work. I may have no teeth by the time Kelly sends help. Power bars long gone. Bunged up on too much white flour. Majorly constipated. Maybe dehydrated too. Drink more. Must have squatted behind trailer for an hour while driving snow filled my flopping pants. Damned snow.

How the hell could Kelly desert me like this? What if he didn't check e-mail? Should've called him.

Forget Kelly. Go for blue light. Just checked. Still there. Brighter yet. Pulsing?

*January 4th*

Found old book by Nipple Mountain expert. Stuffed under old tarps. Should be in museum. Interesting. Wonder how long he stayed up here. Winter? I doubt it. Have to be nuts.

Used up candle reading book. Now what?

> *This journal entry refers to Ryan Bardo's discovery of a doctoral thesis published in 1928 by the Department of Anthropology at the University of Iowa in Iowa City, entitled* On the Shaman's Trail: Reconstructing Early Spiritual Traditions Among the Sunukon Native People of Central Alaska. *The thesis is based on an extensive number of personal interviews with aboriginal elders conducted by Herbert M. Friesen. A remarkably ambitious*

*student, Friesen was apparently well versed in the language of the little known Sunukon people who, due to a devastating flu epidemic, were already in rapid decline by the early 1920s when he conducted his field research.*

*Friesen roamed widely throughout Central Alaska tracking down elders who still spoke the language and knew the ancient stories of this dying tribe. He spent over two years in Alaska, traveling primarily by dogsled or canoe, most often alone. His journeys included a visit to the Nipple Mountain area where he conducted a series of interviews with a former chief and presumed shaman of the local Sunukon. Estimated to be approaching eighty years old, yet living alone in his remote cabin, the man was known as Tchi-chi 'Klo which Friesen roughly translates as "Melter of Snows." The results of Friesen's interviews with Tchi-chi 'Klo are presented in chapter seven of his thesis, "The Sleeping Mother of Nipple Mountain."*

*Not surprisingly, it was this chapter, and this alone, which was of particular interest to Ryan Bardo during his seven days on Nipple Mountain, as indicated by his extensive circling and underlining of numerous sections of text. Though these marked up text excerpts are themselves not in Ryan's own words, they are worthy of inclusion here at some length since they may shed light on his apparent psychological decline and ultimate death. In this regard, the value of these excerpts is amplified when combined with Ryan's hastily penciled remarks in the adjacent margin. These too are included below in their entirety.*

*Here begins the first excerpt marked by the victim.*

The Sunukons' ancient ancestors found enchantment in the nurturing bounty of nature, faced terror in its destructive force, and revered both aspects of their experience as necessary blessings of Sunímah, the Sleeping Mother. Tchi-chi 'Klo emphasized that her story is as relevant today as it was for his ancestors and that her two-edged powers would outlast the very stars. He likened her powers to a double-headed arrow that, in the twinkling of an eye, could just as easily nurture life as take it. When asked by this writer if he had ever witnessed the Sleeping Mother's powers first-hand, Tchi-chi 'Klo stated without hes-itation that not a day goes by when he does not see some evidence of her Lila-chó, which roughly translates as "Great Game." Then, with a slight jut of his chin, he gestured towards Nipple Mountain, adding that the Sleeping Mother was more real to him than this writer.

When asked why Sunímah was always sleeping, Tchi-chi 'Klo stated that the world emerges from her dreams. He explained that her two-edged powers are held in balance by her breaths. Something is born when she exhales. Something dies when she inhales. He said that to lead a safe and

happy life, one must do everything possible to not upset this balance. Only one
thing can do this, he added with a sharp
glance, and that thing is human fear.

*Beside this paragraph Ryan scribbled:* yikes!
Don't mess with her! *He circled the following
excerpt three times.*

Nipple Mountain is an isolated plug
dome of resistant volcanic rock form-
ing a distinctive 300-foot high promi-
nence in an otherwise rolling alluvial
valley. The Yukon River parallels the
eastern flank of Nipple Mountain,
then, about a mile downstream, bends
sharply northward through a short,
fast-flowing canyon. According to
Tchi-chi 'Klo, this segment of the river
may randomly open even on the cold-
est days of winter, emitting great clouds
of chilled vapor. There is no known
hydrological explanation for this phe-
nomenon but Tchi-chi 'Klo explained
that this is a bad omen. The Sunukon
considered the canyon especially
sacred, viewing it as the Sleeping
Mother's womb. The '*sign of the steam*,'
as he called it, indicated that she is '*waking up to the smell of fear running loose on
the land*.' He added that '*sideways snow*'
and '*the smile of a wolverine*' are two
other sure signs of her waking."

*The underlining above was done in Ryan's hand. In the margin he wrote:* Three signs. Waking up. Check out smoking canyon. Wolverines long gone. *The latter comment reflects his well-developed knowledge of local natural history. In* Large Mammals of Alaska *(White Squall Press, 1998), zoologist Manfred Hoyle states that, "There are no known records of wolverine being observed or trapped within approximately fifty miles of Nipple Mountain and the adjacent Yukon River valley since 1931. Research into local aboriginal knowledge and trapping practices might shed light on this unusual extirpation."*

*January 5th*

Getting ridiculous. Hardly slept. Wind just won't die. Damned, screaming wind! Floor booms with every gust. Snow pounded tin walls all night. Sounded like machine gun fire. Now it's hissing through claw marks in door as I write. Can't hack this much longer. What did that guy call it? Sideways snow. Tried to seal cracks. Running out of duct tape. Headache worse. Can't see straight. Might be propane. Must fix leak.

Wolverine dream last night. Scratching somewhere above me. Beside me. Like fingernails on chalkboard. Trying to get in. Crazy! Bandit face in window. All teeth. Must have been dream. Not sure. Second sign?

Don't read that book!

*January 6th*

Fell head first off tower ladder. Brain supernovaed. Conked out. Shivering woke me. Snow in my face. Up my nose. In my mouth. All the snow of the universe. Up my ass.

Run. GET OUT!

*January 7th*

Door crashed in again last night. Ripped right off hinge this time. Splat! Wind kicked it in. What else could??

Ran for tower. Almost blown off ladder. Tower shaking. Swaying. Everything's falling apart. Try to sleep up there. Only safe place. Freeze ass. Snow stops. Wind too. Finally!

That stillness. Cabin light dazzling like blue jewel. Pure sapphire. Then disappears. Then back. Something hides blue light. No! Something moving. Something big. . . . Steam? Third sign. NO WAY!

Back in trailer, same snow claws on floor. Nipple Mother tricks! Cranked heater full blast. Red hot. Claws soon puddles. HAH!!

Idea. . . .

Tower can save me. Old dry wood. Melt snow. Signal fire. Found gas can by junked generator.

I'LL SHOW HER!!

> *With these strange remarks, Ryan's journal ends.*
>
> *Kelly Saunders received Ryan's e-mail too late. Frustrated by prolonged frigid weather over the Christmas holidays, Kelly's family took an unplanned "Last Minute Club" flight to Hawaii on New Year's Day. The Bardo family had no idea where Ryan was until the Saunders returned late on January 11th and Kelly opened Ryan's e-mail. An Alaska Search and Rescue helicopter was dispatched at first light the next morning and reached Nipple Mountain by 0958. The pilot, Mitch Ridder, described the peculiar scene that greeted them in a story published in the Fairbanks Daily News on January 15th.*

I knew something was bizarre when we got within a few miles of the mountain. I couldn't see the fire tower. What a surprise when we discovered it toppled over, right smack on the forestry trailer. That kid must have torched the tower for some reason and down it went.

*The victim was located by aerial search at 1022. He was lying prone, face-down in the snow in an open tamarack forest approximately one mile north of the fire lookout station. His body was frozen solid.*

*The circumstances surrounding Ryan Bardo's death remain a mystery. However, the immediate cause has been confirmed by a gullet to groin autopsy requested by the Alaska Bureau of Investigation. The autopsy report concluded that Ryan Bardo suffocated from "a sudden, high volume inhalation of snow indicated by significant meltwater pooling in the lungs." The report suggests that "a remarkable volume of snow entered the lungs, likely during a violent frontal fall compounded by rapid gasping breaths while running at top speed." It also notes pronounced constriction of the upper air passages, a condition known as "self-strangulation" which may have contributed to his death. This condition was first identified in house-fire victims who succumb to non life-threatening smoke due to an intense panic response.*

*Hypothermia may have been another contributing factor as the victim was wearing only a light cotton jersey, a sweatshirt, blue jeans, and his damaged boots. His goose-down parka, insulated windpants, and other warm clothing items were later found in the trailer, suggesting he made a rushed final exit. The cause of his apparent haste is unknown.*

*Ryan Bardo might have survived another two to three weeks at the Nipple Mountain fire station by combining his outdoor skills with prudent rationing of available food and fuel supplies. In spite of these favorable circumstances, his journal entries suggest that mounting anxiety and restlessness gradually eroded his judgement to the point of jeopardizing his own life. A post-mortem psychological assessment, prepared by Dr. Carl Renner concludes:*

Ryan Bardo's notorious inclination to winter malaise may have reached acute proportions, exacerbated by lack of illumination, loss of his glasses, sleep deprivation, and noxious propane fumes. His growing apprehensions swiftly gained momentum in his last days with the sudden emergence of a further pathology: chionophobia, an irrational fear of snow.

*No evidence was found suggesting the victim was visited by any threatening individual or animal while taking shelter in the station's trailer. However Sam Gulo, the Search and Rescue paramedic who retrieved the body, remarked that there appeared to be two sets of tracks in the snow. In a transcribed police statement given January 13th, he said:*

The kid was obviously in great shape judging by the incredible distance between each footprint. He must have been running full out in spite of the deep snow and his mangled boots. From the helicopter we noticed a weird set of lone tracks that crisscrossed the kid's path like . . . I don't know . . . like something was shadowing him. We followed them back up the mountain a bit. The tracks—big tracks!—looked human near where we'd found the kid. But up higher, near the wrecked fire tower, I'm not kidding, they were definitely made by something on all fours. A bear? A wolf? A wolverine maybe? I don't know. It was really freaky. . . .

*Alaska Fish and Game biologist Barney Scott returned the next day to confirm Gulo's observations but reported that all tracks by the body recovery site had since been erased by blowing snow.*

*Before returning to Fairbanks, Scott flew ten miles northward up the valley to investigate the cabin referred to in the boy's journal, and to which he may have been headed when he died. The only sign of human habitation observed along this stretch of river was a small log cabin located 3.8 miles from the station, where Tusara Creek meets the Yukon's east bank.*

*Scott's helicopter landed here for a site inspection. In his trip report he stated that,*

The cabin was in pretty bad shape. No door in sight and the place was choked with snow. Half of the roof must have caved in long ago. Too dangerous to enter.

*A subsequent review of historic land tenure maps confirmed that this cabin belonged to the Sunukon shaman, Tchi-chi 'K lo and has been unoccupied since his death in 1931.*

*The file of Ryan Bardo remains open pending further investigation by the Alaska State Troopers.*

*−Victor A. Bhaya*
*Coroner, Southeast Fairbanks County*

# X X X X X

*Jamie Bastedo is a naturalist, educator, and broadcaster living in Canada's snowy subarctic. Well established as a popular science writer, he has written six books and over a hundred magazine articles on northern nature. This story was inspired by Jamie's latest book,* Falling for Snow: A Naturalist's Journey into the World of Winter, *in which he explores snow from many angles, some of which are downright creepy. No other element in nature provokes such wildly contrasting emotions as snow— from reverence to revulsion. Get on the wrong side of snow, and you might come down with a bad case of chionophobia, an irrational fear of snow.*

# BEYON·D THE GRAVE

## Diana Aspin

There's a full moon, high above the woods. Chloe will not need a flashlight. She slips into jeans and a sweat-shirt and sets about gathering the things she'll need. Most importantly she needs her mother's sharp spade, the one that breaks through the hardest earth. Then the doggie treats they gave to Max at each of his birthday parties. Still in a green garbage bag in the utility room are Max's red and silver party hat, yellow trumpet, and doggie party boots. These are as old as their golden lab itself: red leather with the silver sparkles she and Jeff had glued on.

As she steps down into the utility room, Chloe knocks her head on the light; the bare bulb swings wildly above her head, casting light on and off the mousetraps by the pressure tank. In one trap is a mouse, cannibalized by another mouse. Its legs are gnawed to the bone, its face is half off; dried foam crusts the corners of its mouth and its broken neck floats in some foul-smelling fluid. Chloe grabs the garbage bag and flees.

Outside, the spade is waiting for her, up against the maple tree, its sharp, silvery cutting edge stuck with soil and baby-fine roots. Chloe's bare feet sink into the damp earth as she drags the bag over to Max's grave. She breathes in deeply the smell of wood smoke and damp earth. Down below, water licks and laps at rocks along the shoreline. She's afraid, and, as sick as it sounds, a little excited by the thought of seeing her old friend again.

No matter what anyone says to her, Chloe knows the accident was her fault. They'd been swimming off the end of the boat, in the narrows behind Bigwin Island. Her dad dozed in the back seat and her mom up front read a book. She and her older brother Jeff dived in, followed, as always, by Max. At some point Max yelped and Chloe turned from climbing onto their green tube. He paddled frantically in her direction. Tossing back his golden head, he yelped again.

"Good boy!" Chloe shouted, above the din of a passing boat. Next thing she knew her mom was screaming, waving her book about like a flag at the finish line. "Jeff! Chloe! Max is in trouble!" By the time they grabbed him and their dad hauled him into the boat, he was groaning horribly, his glossy head, with its trusting yellow eyes and graying beard, lolled to one side, his broad chest heaving. By the time they reached their dock, Max was limp in Chloe's arms, eyes glazed over, dead.

"It was my fault," Chloe cried. Max had begged for his life and she'd turned away. Her mother made her shower and put on pajamas, then gave her some brandy. "You're so high-strung, honey, it's best you sleep."

"No!" Chloe cried, choking on the brandy. "You're always saying I'm high-strung. It was my fault. It was! Leave me alone!" Eventually, though, she'd fallen asleep and not woken until the following morning. During which time her family had decided to spare her the agony of Max's burial. Max, *her* dog, was tucked into the corner of her mom's flowerbed, surrounded by tall poppies and echinacea, weighed down by a slab of quartz-chipped Muskoka rock.

Chloe wept until her eyes were swollen shut. She begged and begged for them to let her see him one last time.

"We can hardly dig him up," her mom said. "Max was a dog, Chloe, not a human being."

Her dad said equally dumb things like, "You engrave the stone. That'll be *your* way of saying goodbye." She hated it when they treated her as though she was four and not fourteen. Just because she'd always been a little "high-strung" as they called it, vulnerable.

Week after week Chloe *tried* to pen an epitaph. Poem after poem, but none of them came out right. None made her feel any less heartbroken, or angry, any less guilty for not saying goodbye. Max must think she'd abandoned him.

Chloe had nightmares. A dark shape skulked in the hemlock wood at the side of the house. It was Max, lake water dripping from his mouth and tail, his eyes eerie beams of orange light. When she called him he slipped away, weaving between the trees. She stumbled into the woods after him but he was smoky, inchoate, always a dog's length ahead. She drank beer to drive away the nightmares but no amount of it did the trick.

Six weeks after Max's burial, their dreaded aunt Lucy came to stay. "Time you grew up, girl. Faced your losses," she carped. Bitch, Chloe thought, and laughed in her face for so long the whole room grew deathly quiet.

That same night, Chloe crawled under the sheets, fully clothed, and pulled the covers up to her chin. She dreamed that she said goodbye to Max in the only way possible. She cradled him in her arms, rocked him, sang to him, babied all the precious parts of him: the liquid velvet of his ears, the broad bones of his forehead, the pads of his paws, the baby-fine hairs of his tummy. She screamed out loud and wept all over him; nobody tried to stop her. She soaked him with tears and snot, said sorry again and again until, in her dream, Max sensed her sorrow deep inside his dead bones and forgave her. After midnight, she was woken by the shrill, final death shriek of a rabbit. Her pillow was drenched with tears, her hair matted to her face. She sat up in bed and stared brutal-eyed at the full moon rising behind the hemlock wood.

The burial stone is larger and deeper than Chloe remembers; it's about the size of two jumbo cereal packages. Chloe leans over, grips the head of it, and tugs. The stone's embedded quartz twinkles in the moonlight; over the past six weeks it has sunk, creating a vacuum between itself and the earth. Little by little, with the tip of the spade, she eases the edges of the stone from the compacted earth. When she pulls again it comes free with a jolt that sends her stumbling backwards. Gasping, she collapses to her knees and heaves it to one side.

Under that dark earth is her dog. *Her* dog. "I'm coming, Max," Chloe whispers. The words she should have shouted that fateful day in the lake—but didn't. She planned to exhume the dog with the spade but now, here on her knees, it seems only fitting that she greet him with her bare hands. She crawls over, and, much like a dog, begins to tear at the compressed earth.

Chloe works a grid, clawing in at one corner, working toward the other, then starting over. It strikes her that it could take until dawn at the rate she's going, slow and steady on all fours, panting. She yearns to see something for her effort. She sits back on her haunches and works out where Max's head might be.

Concentrating on the top left corner she digs deeper and deeper, becoming frantic when her hands meet with only plant roots and the odd stone. She stops once to catch her breath. She thinks she smells the animal dung her mom mixes with the soil. The wind shushes through the massive hemlocks in the wood beside her, then drops suddenly, a silence so utter there's a ringing in her ears. She paws some more and then it happens. The frenzied fingers of her right hand meet something hard.

Rocking back on her heels, Chloe pushes her hair from her face and covers her mouth. She thinks of that mouse in its trap, its leg gnawed to the bone, the pool of rancid liquid beneath its broken neck. This could be the way to more heartache, not less, Chloe hears her know-it-all mother say. She slides onto her belly and slips her fingers back into the pocket of earth they'd left. She can grasp the hard thing between thumb and first finger. It *has* to be a leg. She walks her fingers first up the leg and then down it until she reaches a fan of small bones. *Yes!* She grasps the paw with her whole hand, tight, and lays her cheek on the soil above it. *Max!* And, as though in reply, a twig-snapping, leaf scuttling sound from the silent hemlock woods beside her. From where she is, on her belly, she sees it again, sliding between the trees.

*No! Its feet don't even touch the ground!*

"I'm sorry, Max," Chloe whispers.

*Sorry isn't enough!* She gives the paw a tiny squeeze. *Hang in there, boy. I'm coming.* It buckles in her hand.

Chloe senses the paw scuttle toward her as she lets it slip from her fingers. Energized, she brushes the soil from her face, spits it from her mouth and lips. The moon is full now and will soon begin its inexorable descent. She needs all the light she can get. *Hurry! Hurry!*

Rocking forward onto her hands and knees, Chloe digs for all she's worth. The digging is fast and rhythmic, and the deeper she digs, the more euphoric she becomes. Her heart pumps away inside her chest like a machine; she feels she could go on like this forever. When her fingers hit bone or fur she scrambles on to another area. A fetid stench leaks from the grave reminding her of shit and their next door neighbor's bad breath. She breathes it in, deeply, willingly, for she knows that in a matter of minutes she will have Max in her arms to rock and to sing to, to kiss: the crinkled wet tip of his snout, the pads of his paws, his tummy.

Chloe pants and digs, pants and digs. Soil, along with chunks of fur and flesh, fly. At exactly 4:45 she releases Max from his hellish prison. She drags him onto her lap, embraces him. She can't see him too well; the moon is almost down. Her jeans are stuck with earth, her shirt sodden with sweat. There is grit between her teeth and she tastes earth.

Digging into the garbage bag full of Max's party stuff, she comes up with the red, sparkly hat. She lifts Max's head with one hand. She struggles to get the hat on him with the other but the elastic snaps. She grabs a red boot. The waning moon catches its silvery sparkles. Max's foot slides away from his leg as she lifts it; it slips about inside his ill-fitting skin.

*Carry on! Don't stop!*

Chloe gags. She eases the boot onto the detached foot. When she stops to catch her breath, she sees a shape flit through the undergrowth along the perimeter of the wood. *What is it?* Whatever it is, it makes the sound she heard earlier. Twigs snap. In the still night, leaves rustle.

Hands shaking, she removes the yellow trumpet from the garbage bag. She fishes out the packet of venison treats. Max's head flopped back over her arm, she sprinkles the hard pellets across his grimace of his mouth.

Chloe gasps. She sees, out of the corner of her eye, that movement in the woods again. Something feral, perhaps a raccoon lured by the dog's putrescence. But who is she kidding? When she turns to the woods it's still there. Something amorphous gliding through the trees, its electric-blue imprint fleetingly seared into the space behind it as it proceeds.

With a sudden jolt, Max's skull drops further back, his skin stretching to contain it. The feeling on her arm is, surprisingly, more rousing than repellent. The skulker in the woods must be the spirit of Max reassuring her! *Thank you!* The essence of Max forgiving her!

*Thank you!*

*Thank you!*

Deep in her gut there is an unexpected stirring. She grabs the yellow trumpet and gives it a celebratory blow.

At the hollow sound, dread sweeps through Chloe; it's as though she's tumbled into an abyss. The trumpet clatters onto the headstone. She is disappearing, being swallowed whole, but she fights it. She pulls Max closer. His bones crumple to fit the contours of her chest and lap. She begins to pet him—*okay, boy, okayokayokay.* After all he has forgiven her. That thing trailing its electric blue imprint through the hemlocks is proof perfect of his forgiveness. Max, from beyond the grave, has given her absolution.

Max's skin slips this way and that across his broad forehead as she strokes him. An ear, full of worm holes, comes away in her hand.

*Sorry. Sorry, boy.*

Chloe rubs her cheek. Her fingers are sticky and cold.

Pull yourself together, girl, she hears her aunt Lucy snap.

*Sorry, Aunt Lucy. Can't stop now!*

Max's jawbone comes away in her hand. She's startled but tosses it aside and carries on. Max's joints seem oiled. They float hideously in their sockets. One slithers free of its cradle and she feels it, round and smooth as a ball bearing, through his skin.

Chloe is like a furnace switched on. Heat begins to rise, flames licking into every square inch of her. Her skin sparks. Under the dead weight of Max, her legs tremble. *Sorry! Sorry!* His belly caves in as she strokes it. Her hand plunges straight through him to his backbone, the vertebrae parting like chick peas between her fingers.

Her sudden, visceral appetite for more shocks her.

*I must be mad! Mad!*

Then, as though to confirm it, the creature reappears, stitching up the trees with its sinister blue imprint.

Catapulted to her senses, Chloe leaps up. Flesh, bone and clumps of pelt slither from her lap.

The woods are no longer a collection of trees, earth, and rock but have taken on the menace of human form. "No!" she screams at them. "Leave me alone! Stop it!"

Chloe's sprinting in circles now, yelping, wiping the flesh from her fingers down the sides of her jeans. Her parents and Jeff will hear! She makes a valiant effort to kick Max's corpse into the grave. But there are too many parts to him now and they are, in their shapes and their advanced state of decay, flagrantly uncooperative.

By the time her parents and brother surface Chloe is down at the lake. She's torn off her soiled clothes and hurled herself into the water. It is icy cold against her burning skin. Thrashing and screaming, she rubs the water into her cheeks, shampoos it through her hair. "Help me! Help me!" She pierces the air with her shrieks as she races her hands down her arms and legs, struggles to get the sticky flesh from between her toes and from under her nails while keeping her head above water. She squints through her hair which shrouds her face like a net.

Her dad must have seen the carnage: entrails amongst the poppies, a jawbone buried in the echinacea, on his way down; he stands there, rigid, his shocked face lit by what is left of the moon, his pajama pants flapping in the wind.

"Calm down, sweetie, please," her mom begs, falling to her knees at the end of the dock.

"Hold on, Chloe." Jeff dives to her rescue.

"Jeff!" She never would have thought she could be so relieved to see him.

But her relief is replaced instantly by horror. Through her web of hair, she sees the woods, rising from a cliff of boulders.

A creature—*the* creature—coils between the trees, coming to rest on the highest point of rock. Over her father's shoulder, a pair of ochre eyes mirror the fading moon.

Jeff grabs Chloe's arm and yanks her toward him. "You're okay. Hold still."

With all the strength she can muster, Chloe heels him in the stomach. Away from him she parts her veil of hair. Staring down at her is a wolf-like creature—beast would be a better word—long-snouted, skeletal, its fur rising from its face in matted clumps. It is not a wolf, though. It is not of this world, she knows that now.

"What have you seen?" her mom asks, turning to look. She leans toward Chloe and holds out her blue and pink check blanket. "Come on, honey, you'll catch your death of cold."

Jeff attempts to grab her again and savagely she kicks him away.

"Get away. You can't help me," she cries out.

The creature stares down *at* her, *through* her. Then, like the moon, it begins its slow and inexorable descent. Chloe hears her mom's pleas and feels her brother's shy grab at her arm. The beast rushes by her father, close enough to brush the hem of his pajamas. Chloe feels a rush of uncorrupted terror as her father looks down in alarm and slaps at his ankle.

The beast is at the dock now, next to her mother. It regards her mother dispassionately, then turns its gaze upon her.

The gaze is for her alone. It is mesmerizing, potent, a harbinger of pure evil.

X X X X X

*Diana Aspin was born in Blackpool, England. Her first book,* Ordinary Miracles *(Red Deer Press,*

*2003), was published in 2003. Her short story, "Mom" won a Thistledown Press competition and was published in* Opening Tricks *(1998). Her story, "Deep Freeze," was a runner-up in another Thistledown competition and was published in* Notes Across The Aisle *(1995). She has placed third in the* Toronto Star *Short Story competition and been a runner-up twice. Diana taught short story writing and freefall writing to adults from 1995-2001. She has worked as a waitress, sales assistant, civil servant, office cleaner, cinema usherette, stay-at-home mom, and counselor in a women's shelter.*

# THAT TIME OF THE MONTH

## Joanne Findon

It's happening again. The third month, now. My skin is all itchy and prickly. The tiny hairs on the backs of my hands stand up thick and springy, although they're still invisible. It's getting worse—every part of it. Right now, as I watch the crowded hall around my locker, I can smell everything. Everyone's sweat, whiffs of perfume and stale cigarette smoke, sweet apples inside lunch bags—I can distinguish every single scent, like grains of sand under a magnifying glass. I don't remember noticing that before. Maybe I just wasn't paying attention. Maybe it's being in love. . . .

"Hey, there you are." Tyler slides out of the crowd, slips an arm around me, and pulls me close to kiss me. I breathe in the good smell of him. A whiff of dog mixed in with the aftershave; must be from his dog Rex. Come to think of it, Tyler even looks like a dog, with his hair curling around his ears like that. . . .

"What have you got now?" I ask, pulling away reluctantly.

"English, then nothing. You?"

"Geography." I grimace.

"Meet you at Pizza Paloma after?"

"Yeah."

He kisses me again, long and sweet. Then he's gone.

I turn back to my locker, but something stops me. I look down the hall. It's Camille, staring at me. Camille with her pert little nose and perfect lips. Her face is composed, but the stench of her hatred smashes into me like a wave of scalding coffee. I gasp. I feel the hairs on the back of my neck stand up. Do I growl at her? I don't know. Then she's gone.

I came home early . . . couldn't stay long with Tyler today, don't know why. I'm restless. I can't explain it; this is not like me. I have this wonderful boyfriend! Until today I only wanted to be with him, every single minute. Even last month, and the month before, with this itchy skin thing, I just wanted to be *there with him*. But not this time. I just kept thinking: the moon, the moon. Got to get home.

I told him I had a migraine. I lied to him. I hate that. And he was hurt, I could see it.

The moon is out there, floating above a sea of ground fog. Full tonight.

"Lupa?" I jump at Dad's voice behind me. "I think that plate is likely dry by now," he says, gently prying both plate and dish-towel out of my fingers.

"Oh, sorry! I guess I. . . ."

"Lupa, we have to . . . we've got to talk." His warm hands grip my shoulders, and he turns me around to face him.

"Why?" I look into his eyes. There's that haunted look I've seen so often. It's part of all those half-finished conversations. . . .

"It's . . . seeing you like this . . . it reminds me of your mom. It's happening again, what happened to her. It's happening to you too."

"What's happening? What do you mean?" My heart is pounding. "She ran away with some other guy. That's what you always said. . . ."

Dad looks straight into my eyes. "That's only half the truth. She did run away . . . but. . . ." His hands fall away suddenly. "Damn, I didn't want to have to tell you! I hoped you'd be free of that curse. . . ."

"Curse! What curse?" I grab him. I'm suddenly cold.

He takes a deep breath. "You're a . . . a—damn! I can't!" He pulls away, heading for the door. He stops, turns around, not looking at me. "Just remember, honey: be real careful who you trust, and always, *always* hide your clothes in a safe place, where you can find them later. Your mum must've lost hers . . . I been out there in the bush looking . . . for years."

And then he was gone, on his way upstairs.

Curse? I'm shivering. I turn back to the dishes but the moon fills the window and it's calling my name. It's reeling me in. Full moon.

Before I know it I'm standing on the back deck with my jacket on. My skin is prickling all over now. Somewhere to the west, beyond that last streetlight, a howl rises from the jagged blackness of the trees.

It pulls me like the moon. I'm drifting out across the lawn, across the street. Behind me, in the house, a phone is ringing.

"Lupa?" Dad's voice, melting as it reaches me. "It's for you. Lupa?"

I know it's Tyler but I'm already a world away, at the end of the street where the park borders on the open fields at the edge of town. Beyond that the forest beckons, deep and fragrant. I run across the field, then stop, panting. I step into the trees, and everything changes.

I glide through the underbrush, seeing clearly in the dark. Pungent smells surround me: fallen leaves, a creek, squirrels, the droppings of rats, the scents of larger animals. . . . I hear the sounds of wind and the rustlings of night foragers and the death-cry of a mouse. It's all here, in my nose, in my head, all around me.

I duck under some tangled branches and step out into a clearing. The moon is blazing down on it like there's no place else to shine. I move out of the shadows, scratching my itchy, tingling skin. And then I see the wolves.

There are maybe twenty of them, standing quietly in a crescent, gazing at me with wise, glowing eyes. The largest one steps forward and growls softly. Somehow I know what he means: "You won't be needing those."

I gaze down at my clothes. Slowly I strip: first the jacket, torn now by the brambles, then my shirt, my jeans, my panties. I'm naked in this forest clearing, but I'm not cold. Of course I'm not cold: I've grown fur all over me. Amazingly, this does not astonish me: the itching has stopped. I look down at the jeans at my feet, hear Dad's words like gravel: "Always hide your clothes in a safe place." I fumble with them even as my hands shrink and change to paws without thumbs, and stuff them all underneath a fallen log.

I sit back on my haunches, wrap my tail around my paws. It all feels so perfect, so natural.

The big male takes one long look at me, then lifts his muzzle skyward and howls.

The immensity of that lonely, lovely sound sweeps me up. I lift my head and howl too. Words slip away in the primal chorus echoing against the moon's whiteness. The howl is in me and all around me, pure longing, pure ecstasy, pure song, undiluted, one with the blinding moon.

It's near dawn when I come to myself, curled up on a bed of leaves. There's a taste of salt in my mouth. Phe! I spit out a small bone. There's another wolf with me, warm and soft against my back. I sniff: a female. A memory swirls like smoke. . . .

I remember who I used to be. The clothes! I rise and sniff the ground, follow a clear invisible trail. There they are. I reach in a paw and drag them out. How to put them on? One paw in one sleeve, then the other . . . . As I struggle, I start shivering violently, then notice I have bare skin and arms again. I pull on the muddy shirt and jacket, hurrying and fumbling in the cold. My goose-pimpled legs struggle into damp jeans. I look up, teeth chattering, and see the female gazing at me with steady, sad eyes. She makes a small noise: "Be careful."

"I will." I shove my feet into muddy shoes and head back through the woods, through the wreaths of mist.

Dad has left the back door unlocked. I pull off my clothes and fall into bed.

I'm floating just beneath the surface of sleep. Voices.

"No, sorry. . . . She's still sleeping. Had a bad night." Dad's voice.

"That migraine still?" Tyler's voice: edgy, poised between annoyance and concern.

"Yeah. Pretty tough on a person. Doubt she'll be going today."

Footsteps, then a car door clunking. The engine's roar. Then quiet.

When I wake up, Dad's gone to work. That salty taste is still in my mouth. Blood? There's a wisp of memory . . . I stumble to the bathroom, grip the edge of the sink, and retch. The worst thing is the bits of animal hair stuck between my teeth. I floss like crazy and rinse my mouth with glass after glass of mouthwash.

After a long, hot shower, I realize my skin isn't itchy anymore. It feels . . . okay.

One night a month. Only one night. Can I live with that?

I'm back at school the next day. Tyler's all tender and sweet again, like nothing ever ripped a hole in our days together.

Camille is nowhere to be seen, and my sense of smell is back to normal. No nasty surprises. Normal: I savor it.

I learn to read the calendar for the full moons. I mark each one at home and make sure I've got something booked for those nights: a friend's band concert, an overnight trip to Toronto to see my aunt, a visit to Grandpa in the nursing home with Dad. Good thing the full moons aren't always on the same day of the week.

But oh, those nights in the moonlight. Each time it's harder to come back, to leave the bright, fierce simplicity of fur and flesh and howling song. Harder to come back to school, to lies, to complications, to Tyler, who seems to want more and more of me . . .

After three months of smooth escapes, I'm caught. It's a Thursday, and I've been so busy with school projects I've forgotten to check the calendar.

"How about a movie tonight?" Tyler breathes in my ear, pulling me close. I inhale his wonderful scent, then realize with a shock that I can smell everything again—just like I always can the day of the full moon.

"Uh . . . no, sorry," I stammer, pulling away, not looking at him. "History. That big project . . . I've got to get it done tonight."

"I've got my geography thing to do. We can work on our stuff together. Order in a pizza. Your place or mine?"

My heart is pounding. "That would be great, Ty . . . but I . . . I have to get a bunch more books at the library downtown, and I'd rather. . . ."

I look up at him just in time to see Camille glide around the corner, her tiny perfect nose in the air as if she's sniffing the wind. She stops and gazes at Tyler, not me. This time her scent speaks not of hatred, but of something else. She wants him. She wants Tyler for herself.

He doesn't see her. He's looking down at me in frustration. "What is it with you sometimes?" he snaps.

I draw back: Tyler *never* snaps, not at anyone. He's the school pussycat.

"You're hot and cold!" he rages. "All sweet and lovey one minute, then you go weird on me for a couple of days. What *is it?*"

I glance past him, scenting danger. Camille slides on down the hall, a smirk on her face. Sticking that pert little nose of hers in where it's not welcome. How does she always know when we're together?

"I. . . ." I stop, breathing hard. I can't tell him. I *must not* tell him!

He tips my chin up and gazes into my eyes. "Lupa, please."

"I wish I could, Ty—but I can't."

"Can't? Or won't?"

"Can't. Really, truly, Ty. *Please* don't ask me any more. It's—it's nothing. I just need time to myself sometimes, that's all."

The scent of his angry frustration is suddenly choking me. I have to get away, I have to breathe!

I slam my locker shut and turn away from him. "I gotta go," I mutter, and hurry down the hall to my next class.

I sit there trying to listen to the geography teacher, but it's no use. I can't think anymore. I have to get away, get away, get away. . . . The words are pounding in my head like a drumbeat.

I bolt from the school as soon as the bell rings and walk home by myself. The stink of car exhaust is better than those human smells, the smells I shouldn't be able to recognize. It takes me ages to get home, but there is comfort in the growing gloom. Sometimes it's safer to be alone.

Dad's not home yet. I flick on the light in the kitchen and put on the kettle to make tea, scratching absently at my tingling skin. I pour the tea and stare at the curl of steam rising from the cup. Beyond it, out the window, the moon breaks free of the distant trees and sings my name.

I grab the edge of the counter and hold on for dear life, but it's no use. I'm out the door before I know it, down the street to the field, to the woods, as if pulled by an invisible hand. The howling has begun already.

I crunch through the underbrush to the clearing, peel off my clothes with fumbling hands, paws, claws. A whisper of cold air on my naked skin before the fur covers it completely. Then a flick of my hind legs to toss the rumpled heap of clothes into a hollow—and there I am. Words melt away. There is nothing but the moment, the wolves, and the moon.

In unison, we sing our ancient chorus. The moon's bright face smiles down at us with kindly wolf eyes. The female draws near me, as usual. We howl together.

Suddenly the wind shifts and I catch a new scent. Human! I stop my song abruptly. One by one, the others fall silent. The great male faces the forest behind me and utters a low, menacing growl. Through our sudden silence floats the soft sounds of human footfalls in the underbrush. The wind brings me two different scents, not one. My hackles rise. Male and female humans. Danger! I growl. The others lift their heads and catch the scent too, draw the circle closer around me.

I know them before I see them. I know the scents of their bodies better than their names now, but both slivers of knowledge enrage me. It's Camille, and with her is Tyler!

They don't see or hear us. Camille is holding a flashlight.

"Look! What's that?" Camille hisses as she leads the way into the clearing, pointing the flashlight at the ground.

"Hey, someone's clothes!" says Tyler, bending down.

In an instant I am pure rage. I spring at Camille and knock her flat. I hear the wind whoosh out of her. She lies there beneath my paws, stunned and breathless; then she begins to scream. Her fear and hatred fill the air around me with their putrefying stench. It makes me crazy.

I growl and bare my teeth. My beastliness is pure, raw joy to me. I want to tear her throat out . . . but then I see that pert little nose of hers silhouetted in the fierce moonlight. Her eyes are wide and glassy with horror. Saliva drips from my open jaws onto her exquisite, terrified face.

Then I bite her nose off.

Camille's shrieks pierce the moonlight. The other wolves bound near and surround us. In my mouth I savor the saltiness of the blood, the smooth contours of the bleeding nose. My long wolf's tongue rolls it around for a few delicious moments. Then I let it drop onto her breast. I raise my muzzle to the sky and howl. Then I leap off her and bound into the forest. Other wolves follow me, but the male remains behind, growling at the two of them.

"Oh my God!" shouts Tyler "Oh my God! Camille!"

As I run, I hear another voice behind him, fainter. Dad's voice.

I rush on, and soon there is nothing but the wolves and the trees and the quiet dark, and the moon filling the whole world.

It's near dawn when I return to the clearing. It's empty now. I sniff all around and find the spot where Camille lay. Blood has soaked into the damp leaves, but that's the only trace of her. Of *them*. The scent of danger rises from that blood. Danger to me.

I sniff for my clothes, filled with sudden dread that they've been taken. The female wolf has followed me, and she helps me search. Finally we find them—folded up in a small square and tucked neatly just inside a burnt-out stump. I paw them out, then stop.

Is that what I really want? Suddenly I'm reeling between the scent of the human clothes and the tapestry of forest smells. The female wolf gazes at me. I know who she is. I could stay. I *want* to stay. A longing as big as the moon seizes me.

"Go," she growls, nuzzling me once, gently. "Go."

I turn slowly and slip my front legs inside the sleeves. As the grey light seeps into the forest, I recover my fingers and my bare skin. Carefully I do up the buttons on my shirt, slide my human feet into my shoes as the human thoughts slide into my brain and I realize fully what danger I'm in. To be hunted here, or hunted there: that is my choice. I gaze back at the female.

Her sad eyes meet mine. "Go," she growls again.

"Goodbye," I say, almost choking on the word.

She watches me solemnly as I turn and head back to the house.

Dad is sitting at the kitchen table, warming his hands on his coffee cup. He looks up and smiles a weary smile.

"She'll be okay," he says. "Plastic surgery's pretty good these days."

I sink into my chair, cradle my head in my hands. "I never meant to—"

"Hush," Dad says, laying a hand on my shoulder. "They'll be looking for a wolf, not a teenager. But you gotta be extra careful now."

"I know."

He scrapes at his cup with one fingernail, runs a hand through his hair. "D'you think. . . ." he mutters, "D'you think . . . you'll be able to keep coming back?"

I sigh and stare out the window at the sunrise. "I don't know, Dad." I get up and give him a big hug. "I don't know."

## X X X X X

*Joanne Findon grew up in Surrey, British Columbia. She has spent years studying medieval history and literature and writing stories inspired by times past. Her first picture book,* The Dream of Aengus, *a retelling of a medieval Irish tale, won the Toronto IODE Award.* Auld Lang Syne *is a non-fiction picture book about Scottish poet Robert Burns.* When Night Eats the Moon *(Red Deer, 1999) is a time-travel fantasy novel for young adults set in modern-day England and prehistoric Stonehenge. "That Time of the Month" was inspired by a medieval werewolf tale. Joanne teaches English literature at Trent University. She lives in Peterborough, Ontario, with her husband and daughter.*

# Consequences

## Sylvia McNicoll

The huge, white moon throws my shadow on the road a couple of hundred meters below, giving me a preview of how my body will look implanted there. A truck runs over it and I swallow hard. The wind hoots through the underpass, laughing like my father. "Trouble with you is you've got no backbone." Is that a thought of my own or something he once told me? The road blurs as I totter slightly. I wave my arms for balance and manage to stay standing on the railing.

A figure in the center lane down there waves. Dark gray suit, burgundy tie—Dad? Can't be. He's dead. I know because I killed him myself right on that spot where he's standing. What does the arm waving mean? Is he copying me or trying to stop me? I can see his lips move but his voice comes from inside my head.

"Go ahead, jump. You'll never amount to anything, you worthless piece of crap."

The voice I always hear, day in, day out. I need to stop it. I take a deep breath and jump.

They say if you drop a penny from the CN Tower onto someone's head, the speed at which it falls will increase the impact so that it will slice right through their skull and kill them. It's an idea that always intrigued me. I used to throw tomatoes from the overpass. The same tomatoes Dad grew and used to let ripen on the garage floor in the late fall. "Fresh tomatoes, fresh basil, what you put into your pot, you get on your plate," my father's version of "You are what you eat." They became sauce either way, except I hated my father's spaghetti. I liked the tomatoes much better as a splash of red on the highway.

Or on cars, white especially. On yellow school buses, the tomatoes looked pretty gruesome too—which gave me the idea that eventually killed Dad.

It was getting close to Halloween and I was in a bad mood because I didn't have any money to get a costume. The school was having a dance and I thought if I dressed in one those store-rented costumes I might impress Serena, the long-legged new girl from England. I asked Dad for a loan—I mean, he was the Rossi in the law firm, Rossi, Reynolds and Rogue, it wasn't like he couldn't shell out a few extra bucks over and above my allowance.

"You get everything too easy. Go out and get a job. When I was your age I had paper routes . . . not just one . . . I organized a bunch of kids to deliver for me."

Same old story.

"What if I wash the car?" Dad loves his Status looking clean and shiny.

"Not some half-assed job like you did last time. The moon window too. And the lights."

"I'll vacuum the inside and wash the floor mats."

"I don't know if I trust you. Last time I found a scratch near the gas cap."

"That was the guy at the gas station, I keep telling you."

"Fine. Twenty bucks. Take it or leave it. For thirty I can get it professionally done. You have to do it for less to get my business."

Dad's Status never looked better. That red paint glowed like a sunset. I'd even put a little of that eucalyptus oil he likes so much on the inside of the car so it smelled like a koala bear's paradise too.

I went to the costume store on Main Street and looked for something that might impress Serena. There was a sale on Santa Claus—no more Frankenstein or Grim Reaper—and a devil's costume that was dorky. But I thought the knight outfit was cool. A little complicated to go to the bathroom but the guy showed me the secret trap door in the armour. A hundred bucks. Way too much, but I knew I had to have it. I put down my deposit. The twenty dollars I'd spent all of Sunday earning.

For the rest of the money, I had to put the squeeze on the geeks and dweebs at the school. It wasn't so hard really. At St. Michael's High we had a cafeteria. Kids hate bringing sandwiches for lunch so they're always loaded up with cash to buy food. I heard Dad's voice in my head "Canadian kids are too fat anyway. Won't hurt if they miss a meal." So I started with Blubber Boy, Donovan White, slamming an arm lock on him till he handed me his wallet. Next day I pumped ketchup on porky Ryan Philips when he was slow paying and after that I just worked my way down through Elephant Alex and the other lard butts to the smaller guys. Day three Jamie Terrino handed me five dollars before I even asked, but I still ploughed him into the locker hard enough for the vents to make an imprint on his forehead. "It'll make a man of the little pansy," I thought, something my father regularly said about me to my mother.

In a couple of weeks I'd gathered about sixty bucks in protection money. So close, just another twenty dollars. I got tense and maybe a little careless. When Danny Fryes the crybaby came to school empty-handed, I dumped him upside down in the can. Something Dad did to me once when I swore at him. "I'm your father. Show some respect."

I only saw the drooley-mouthed CP kid at the doorway after I was done. Not that it should have mattered. He can't do anything anyway. He can't feed himself or talk clearly. "Who would want to live like that?" Dad would say. Someone should put a pillow over the kid's head.

Turns out the kid can move the lever on his motorized wheelchair and type messages on a bliss board. He must have used that board to get Mr. Fallows out in time to catch me. Mr. Fallows gave me a lecture and a suspension and Dad had to pick me up from the office.

Dad didn't even want to hear my side of the story. When we stepped out of the principal's office, he just walloped me across the face. "You break a rule, that's life; you get caught, that's stupid." Serena happened to be standing there. I saw the look on her face. I had turned into some kind of freak in her eyes. I hated that more than the pain from the slap. More than the grounding which would cost me the Halloween dance—and I now had the hundred bucks for the knight's costume too.

I slid into the Status, tasting salty acid in my mouth coming from where my cheek had cut against my tooth. It trickled from the corner of my lip.

"Don't bleed on the car." Dad handed me a tissue.

That's when the idea came to me.

I knew when and where Dad went for lunch. I'd wait patiently at the overpass. Even if it took a couple of hours, it would be worth it. I'd drop the tomatoes on the roof of the Status.

Red on red. As I walked to the overpass, tomatoes stuffed in my pocket I realized that wouldn't have the best effect. It was

Halloween and the nearby houses all had their pumpkins out. I grabbed one. Much better. Orange flesh splattered all over the Status. He wouldn't know what hit him and I'd take off so fast that he'd never know it was me.

Halloween was an unusually warm day; no snowsuits wrecking the kiddy costumes, I thought as I waited up there from 11:30 on. I kept my eyes trained on the road, my fingers drum-rolling along the railing. Dad's lunch started at noon which gave me time to worry. What if another car came that looked just like it? What if my aim was off? What if someone saw me first? Right on schedule at 12:10 the sun glinted off the Status as it traveled toward me. I held on to the pumpkin till just the right moment and released it as the nose of the car peaked out from under the overpass.

The moonroof was open.

Who could have predicted? I expected the pumpkin to splatter all over the Status wrecking the lovely wax job I had given it. I didn't expect it to hit Dad's head and grind it into his spinal cord.

I never meant for it to happen.

At the funeral, everyone said nice things about Dad. I couldn't imagine any of them being true. People told me to go ahead and cry but I didn't feel like it. My mom looked sad but she made me pile all Dad's stuff on the curb for the diabetes pickup the week after. I nearly puked when I smelled his eucalyptus aftershave coming from the boxes. Next day I heard Mom singing in the kitchen for the first time ever. I sang along.

But I never wanted to kill him. I told him that when he first appeared in my dreams with his head pushed down into his chest.

"Oh, come on, Joe. Just tell me for once in your life you did something and got it right. You saw the roof open and you dropped the pumpkin just so."

"No, never."

"You're pathetic. You'll never amount to anything," he told me as he pulled his head up so that his neck appeared again, vertebrae by vertebrae. It made a knuckle cracking sound and I wanted to be sick.

Then in the daytime I began hearing his voice, just the way I did when he was alive.

"Don't slouch!"

"Any bozo could have done better on that test."

"Are you going to let that kid talk to you like that?"

I couldn't stand it. I put my hands over my ears but I couldn't get away from his words.

Every day, every night.

Finally I screamed at him in my sleep. "Leave me alone!"

"Don't want to listen to your old man anymore, Joe? Then for once in your life, just do the right thing. End it. Show some backbone. There's no future for you anyway." Once again he lifted his head so that his neck appeared.

I sat up in bed and rubbed my eyes hard to get rid of him. But I could still hear him. "Go on. Get your ass out of bed. There's no one at the overpass now. You can get it over with." That's why I went back there in the middle of the night. That's why I jumped.

My eyelids flutter open to brightness and a disinfectant smell. I smile. Just a bad dream. I'm awake now and don't hear Dad's voice at all. Why did I want to jump off the overpass anyway? Life is a lot better without him. No one to yell or hit me.

A fly buzzes in front of my face, so close I can feel the whirring wings tickle past my nose. I reach up to scratch it. Nothing moves. I swear I'm lifting my arm and moving my fingers. I look down but they're lying there motionless as though they belong to someone else. I lift the other one. Same thing.

I blink again. This isn't my room. It's too blank. I hear some quiet voices just outside the room. "Coming out of the coma . . . breathing on his own . . . never walk again . . . never regain upper mobility."

Inside my head, I hear another voice. "Couldn't do one thing right, could you, son?"

I want to tear open my skull to get rid of it.

I shudder at the knuckle crunching noise as Dad straightens his neck out again.

"You just screwed up and created a big vegetable. A pumpkin."

No, no, it can't be. I try to cover my ears with my hands but again nothing moves.

"You've got no backbone."

## X X X X X

*Born in Ajax, Ontario, Sylvia McNicoll grew up an avid horror reader in Montreal, Quebec where she earned a BA in English and Economics at night and invested money for a corporation by day. She began writing after staying home to raise her three children and now has over twenty-two books published in six different languages. She's won the Silver Birch Award, the Manitoba Young Reader's Choice, the Explora-Toy Novel of the Year, and many Our Choice citations from The Canadian Children's Book Center. Characters from her novels* Grave Secrets *and* Grave Consequences *inspired her short story* "Consequences."

# ΠEW FISH

## Wendy A. Lewis

D uncan dumped his backpack in the front hall and headed straight for his room. He wanted to avoid maternal entrapment and also check on his new fish, a Siamese fighting fish he called Flash.

"That you, darling?" his mother called.

The temptation was great to reply, "No, it's the creature from the black lagoon," but Duncan's mother had a different sense of humor. Sometimes, no sense of humor. So "Hi, Mom" is all he said before closing his bedroom door.

Duncan's walls and ceiling were painted dark blue, and used to be covered with star stickers, but most of them had peeled off. He'd been thinking of painting his room black, but since he got Flash, he thought he might live with the blue a while longer. It was kind of like being underwater. Maybe he'd paint a giant squid or something. Something not pink. The rest of the house was pink, although his mom called it "blush," "berry," or "rose" depending on the room. She believed pink had a calming effect on people, but it did the opposite to Duncan. In Pink World, he felt trapped inside a translucent bubble of gum where his mother constantly watched him, exclaiming how much bigger, hairier, and smellier he was growing by the day.

From his bowl on the night table, Flash waved his regal fins.

"Hey, buddy. Hungry?"

Duncan tapped a pellet onto the water's surface. Flash gulped it down and belched out a bubble.

"Have a good day, Flash?"

Flash ejected a turd.

"Yeah, that pretty much sums up my day too."

Duncan's mother knocked on his door and opened it without waiting for an answer.

"Hi sweetie. You were in such a hurry to get up here . . . Is everything okay?"

"Yeah, fine."

"I smell chlorine. Did you go swimming?"

Duncan nodded. Phys. Ed. had been last period of the day, a nightmarish session of swimming with the girls' class. Having to appear half-naked in front of the girls was bad enough; then the guys started calling him "Hairy Tits." Mr. Kilman had shown no mercy either, making him swim lengths until he was gasping for air. Duncan was a weak swimmer. Maybe that's why he liked to watch Flash swim so effortlessly around his bowl.

"You should shower with soap after you go swimming, honey. Chlorine is so hard on your skin."

Right, thought Duncan. Shower with a bunch of guys trying to grab his "hairy tits"? They wouldn't have done that if Randy was still around. What a boon it had been having Randy for a friend. Everybody—guys, girls, even teachers—liked Randy. And when Duncan was with him, people treated him okay. But Randy had moved to California two months ago, and was so busy surfing or skating or whatever it is people do in California that he'd only managed to write once.

"Here's your mail, darling." Duncan's mother handed him a renewal notice for his sci-fi magazine. "Sorry, there wasn't anything from Randy again. I'm really surprised at him—"

"He's busy, Mom. It's no problem."

"Well, if it helps, I know what you're feeling. It's so hard for the person left behind. . . ."

*Please don't tell the Roger story*, Duncan tried to say telepathically. But the Roger story was told. Having heard it a few hundred times since his Mom's last boyfriend was transferred to Vancouver (and his affections transferred to a Vancouver girlfriend), Duncan tuned out and watched Flash instead. Poor guy, it took him all of two seconds to swim a lap of his bowl. On each circuit, he rolled his eyes at Duncan as if to say, *This Roger story gets longer every time she tells it.*

Three more circuits. More eye rolling. Willie at the pet shop said Siamese fighting fish, or bettas, didn't need much space, but Duncan was sure he'd love a bigger container, with some stuff put in to make it more interesting, because staring at the same four walls could drive a guy crazy—he should know!

"—that fish," his mother sighed loudly.

"Pardon?"

"I said, you sure like that fish."

Flash was Duncan's first pet. His mother hated animals and had never let him bring one in the house. She thought dogs and cats were too hairy, birds were too noisy, reptiles belonged in a zoo, and anything resembling a rodent should be exterminated. The only pet she would allow was a fish in a small bowl—no aquariums that might leak and cause expensive water damage—just a nice, boring goldfish in a nice, boring bowl. Thanks but no thanks, Duncan had always said. Until he saw the Siamese fighting fish at the new pet shop in town. There were six bettas lined up in plastic cups with lids. Five of them just hung in the water looking fancy, but the dark blue one—Flash—had waved his fins wildly at Duncan as if he was sending a semaphore message, "Buy *me*."

"Are you going out tonight, sweetheart?"

Yeah, where? Duncan shook his head "no."

"Well, there's a good movie on TV tonight. . . ."

If Duncan's mom thought a movie was good, that meant it was either a chick flick or a disease-of-the-week feature. She loved watching those, and after, watching Duncan for symptoms. The urge to get away, out of the house, was suddenly overwhelming.

"Actually, Mom," he said, standing so fast he felt dizzy, "there's something I wanted to get downtown. I'll see you later."

In seconds he was out the front door, breathing in the crisp October air. He walked without a clear destination in mind, although in a town this size there weren't many places to go. In a few minutes, he found himself standing outside the new shop, *Willie Peacock's Pets*, where Willie was busy creating a new window display. It was supposed to look like an aquarium, but everything was super-sized. The aquarium gravel was the size of fists, the plants were like jungle foliage, the treasure chest was the size of a coffee table and the human skull looked so real that Duncan felt his stomach lurch.

With his orange satin shirt and gold necklaces, Willie was the kind of person Duncan had only seen on TV. Music thumped through the glass, that old song where the guy singing sounds like his privates are in a vice grip: "STAYIN' ALIVE, STAYIN' ALIVE, I, I, I, I'M STAYIN' A-LIIIIIIIIIIIIII-VE!" Willie was singing along energetically as he hung a large papier-mâché betta with invisible fishing line. He motioned for Duncan to come in, but Duncan wasn't sure he could face so much flamboyance right now. Willie wouldn't take no for an answer.

"Come in, come *in!*" he sputtered, pulling Duncan through the door. "I want to hear how it's going with your fish! I never saw such a perfect match between animal and human as you two!"

Saliva bubbled at the corners of Willie's mouth, he was so excited, just as he had been on the day Duncan bought Flash. He smelled of grape bubble gum, which he seemed to be constantly chewing—his "shameful addiction" is how he referred to it during Duncan's first visit.

"I was thinking," Duncan said, accepting a piece of gum from Willie, "that Flash might like a bigger space."

"Hey, what guy wouldn't love more space, huh? Let me show you what I've done with mine. . . ."

"You have your own betta?"

"Two—a blue and a red," Willie said as he led Duncan to the back of the shop.

"I didn't think you could keep them together."

"You can't, not in the same container. They'd tear each other apart! Here they are. Say 'hi,' boys."

On a table sat two tall, curvy glass containers. Willie ran his hands along them and the fish inside swam up, flaring their gills.

"Flash does that," said Duncan.

Willie laughed. "That means he really, really likes you. Actually, it means he wants to mate."

"Oh!"

"I guess when females are scarce, even a finger looks attractive, eh?"

Embarrassed, Duncan didn't answer. The tall, curvy glass made him think of Kim, a girl from swimming class this afternoon.

"Do you sell these containers?"

"None this big. These are vases for flowers, actually. Do you have one at home?"

Duncan knew his mom had one somewhere, left over from the Roger days. He bought a small castle, skull, and plastic plant from Willie, and headed back home, where he found the vase in the china cabinet. He was polishing it with his shirttail when his mother came in the room.

"What are you doing with that?" she asked, somewhat sharply.

"I—I wondered if I could use it? If that's okay . . .?"

"Oh, honey. . . ." Her voice and face softened. "Of course you can! Shall I run the water? Lukewarm water is best—"

"I know, but I'll do it upstairs. Thanks, Mom!"

In his room, Duncan nestled the castle, skull and plant into some marbles in the base of the vase, then filled it with water from the bathroom tap. He'd have to let it sit for a day to make sure it was the right temperature, but he set the vase beside Flash's bowl so Flash could see it.

"What do you think, buddy?" he said.

Flash flared his gills and blew a bubble, which floated to the surface and clumped alongside several others. Willie had told him that male bettas will make "bubblenests" on the water's surface in anticipation of mating and becoming a dad.

"Hate to disappoint you, buddy," Duncan said, "but there's no way my finger's gonna lay eggs."

Undaunted, a guy with a mission, Flash belched out more bubbles.

"Di-nner, darling!" Duncan's mom called.

Whatever his mom had been cooking, it smelled good. Unfortunately, it was also pink. Salmon loaf. Duncan thought his mom had served fish for dinner more than usual since Flash had joined the household. Wishful thinking?

He removed the sprig of parsley, took a bite, and gave his mom a thumbs up.

"Darling," his mother said, "isn't something missing?"

Duncan looked at the table. Salt and pepper, napkins, cutlery—it was all there.

"Don't you notice something different?" she said.

Oh boy. He hated when she played these games. Was her hair different? It was always important to comment favorably if something changed on the hair front. . . .

"There, silly." His mother pointed to a piece of lace on the table.

"You got me," said Duncan. "What's that?"

"A *doily*, silly, for the vase. Don't you think you ought to bring it down now?"

Without Flash in it? And did his mom really want Flash sitting on the table while they ate? From the first day he got Flash, his mother said how revolting it was that he breathed the same water he pooped in.

"The vase, darling?" she said.

Then it hit him. She thought he'd bought flowers for her and borrowed the vase to put them in! She thought he was hiding them up in his room right now, waiting for the perfect time to give them to her. Oh man! His mind raced through possible solutions. Go upstairs, sneak out a window, run to the flower shop, and make it back before dinner got cold. Uh-unh. Better tell her the truth before he dug himself any deeper.

"Mom, I'm real sorry, but I didn't buy flowers, if that's what you thought."

His mom did what Duncan inwardly called "the about-face." He was never sure how she did it. Nothing physical changed as far as he could tell, no muscles moved, her expression seemed to be the same. But it was as if someone slammed a door shut. Wham! Happy hour's over. Mom's different now, and it's because of you, buddy. Duncan sighed.

"I didn't think you'd bought flowers," she said curtly. "Why on earth would you buy flowers? You *never* buy flowers."

Duncan suddenly remembered a hilarious evening at Randy's house, when Randy's mom had put on a Neil Diamond record and started singing that song, "You Don't Bring Me Flowers Anymo-o-o-re. . . ." She had really hammed it up, squeezed out tears, the whole bit. Duncan and Randy had been her back-up singers, clutching their broken hearts as they sobbed out "boo-hoo."

"How *could* you?" Duncan's mother said.

"What?"

"How could you *laugh* at me?"

"I wasn't laughing at you, Mom."

"You *laughed!*"

"I was thinking of something else—"

"I'm clearly upset and trying to *talk* to you and you think of *something else?*"

"Mom . . . I'm sorry." What else could he say?

Duncan carried his plate to the kitchen and set it on the counter carefully, so his mother wouldn't interpret the noise as a slam. Then he went to his room and calculated how many years he had to wait before he graduated from high school and could move out. Maybe he could go to California and live with Randy.

Duncan watched Flash investigate, as much as he was able to, the contents of the vase sitting next to him. He seemed especially interested in the skull; his tail fin flapped energetically from side to side, like a dog sniffing roadkill. The skull was about the size GI Joe's would be, if GI Joe had a skull. For a moment, Duncan really missed Randy. They used to discuss stupid stuff like: if GI Joe's entire unit was gunned down, would he still wear that look of rock-solid calm? Duncan placed his forehead against the cool glass.

"If you had a fish friend," he whispered to Flash, "what would you talk about?"

*Not much.*

Duncan jerked his head back. He hadn't heard the words in his head so much as felt them. And they weren't even words. *Not much* was a pale translation of the sensation that had filled his head. What he felt was absence rather than substance, a complete absence of noise, clutter, and worry. What he felt, for a split-second in that emptiness, was happiness.

Duncan put his face back to the glass. Flash seemed to be smiling. Was Flash happy? Did Duncan somehow tap into that? Not much. Is that what was going on inside Flash's little fish brain? Is that why he was happy? You would be happy, wouldn't you, if you didn't have to worry about over-emotional mothers and bullies at school and friends who ignored you?

Duncan turned off the light and crawled under his duvet. By the light of the moon that shone in his window, he watched Flash swim effortlessly around and around. . . .

That night Duncan dreamed that he was a fish, and for the first time, swimming filled him with joy. He shot to the surface, dove to the bottom, turned somersaults underwater! It was easy! And he didn't feel like half the pool was up his nose! That's because he didn't have a nose—stupid, inefficient things. He had gills, of course. And fins—long, fancy fins like Flash's, only red. I'm a red, Duncan thought! And as soon as he thought it, a blue swam into his field of vision.

*Flash?* Duncan tried to say, but no words came out.

It looked like Flash, but he wasn't looking friendly. He was all puffed up, demanding a fight. Duncan had never fought, but he knew he could do it, now that he had this new body. He lunged at the blue, shredding its tail fin with a chomp of his jaws and twist of his head. . . .

For most of the night, Duncan dreamed of the fight, but there was never a clear winner. Duncan, the red, would seem to be winning, then the blue would flip him over and the tussle would begin again. He was exhausted when he woke the next morning. In his bowl on the night table, Flash hung limp in the water.

"Flash!"

Flash woke up and waved his fins.

"Scared me there, buddy." Duncan sat up, groaning. His head ached.

Flash swam over to study the skull again through the two panes of glass.

"You want to get at that thing, don't you?" Duncan said. Flash flared his gills.

He put one hand on the bowl and the other on the vase. They both felt gloriously cool. The vase had plenty of room for the water that was currently in Flash's bowl, so instead of going across the room to get the net (he felt too tired to anyway,) Duncan merely tipped the bowl and Flash dove gracefully into his new home. He loved it, Duncan could tell. He could almost feel Flash's reaction: *WOW!* Flash sniffed the skull, circled the castle, and wove between the fronds of the plastic plant. Then he did it all again and again and again . . . Duncan watched, smiling. . . .

*"DUNCAN!"*

Flash disappeared behind the castle. Duncan's mother was marching across the room.

"You don't have to yell." Duncan's voice cracked.

"Don't have to yell? I've called you ten times."

"You did?"

"Yes!"

"Sorry."

His mother shook her head at the vase. "I should have known it was for him," she sighed.

Duncan didn't reply. Nothing he could say could make the situation better.

"I trust you've had a good sleep in? I have to go grocery shopping. Is there anything in particular you want me to get?"

Duncan's mind was blank except for one item.

"Bubbles," he croaked.

*"Bubbles?"*

He knew it didn't make sense, but he wanted them, needed them.

"Yeah, uh, bubble stuff . . . you know . . . you blow it. . . ."

Duncan's mother frowned. He whispered the magic word.

"Please . . .?"

Her face softened. "Well . . . I doubt they'd have it at this time of year, but I can check the sale aisle. Are you feeling all right, honey? Throat sore?"

Duncan nodded, but it wasn't a sore throat so much as a sore brain. It was as if the place where his words came from had posted an *Out of Order* sign.

"You're warm," his mother said, feeling his forehead. "Stay in bed and rest, okay? I'll see you later."

As always, she left the door open, but Duncan was too tired to get up and close it. This didn't feel like any cold he'd had before. He felt . . . outside himself. Flash had slowed down too. He had wedged himself between two fronds of the plant and was perfectly still.

*Peace.*

Again, it was a sensation more than the word filling Duncan's mind. Was it Flash doing that? Impossible. It was Duncan's thought, Duncan's alone. Because as peaceful as it must be between the soft fronds of the plant, it was better here in bed with flannel sheets and a down duvet. Ahhh . . . Duncan slept again.

He slept through his mom coming home and checking his temperature with the ear thermometer. He slept through dinner—leftover salmon loaf. He slept through the telephone ringing. It was Randy, calling from California. His mother said Duncan was sick and taking a nap. Randy said he'd call in a day or so, when Duncan was better.

While Duncan slept, he dreamed he was a fish with long, powerful fins that propelled him through the water at fantastic speeds. He bore the scars that had earned him the title of Siamese Fighting Fish, and his reputation spread so far that other males hid when he glided past. These other males stuck to their own small territories, their own small lives, but he explored the waterways of his world. He explored rice paddies, circling the ankles of the two-legged creatures that stumped awkwardly along. He explored rivers, where castles towered and poles displayed gruesome heads, the ragged flesh peeling away to expose the skulls beneath. He mated with every female he met. No one turned him down. They were every color, size, and age, too many to remember. Nest-building, seduction, fertilization, incubation, fatherhood . . . Duncan refined it to an art that he executed swiftly and competently before he moved on.

In his dream, he was aware that he had once existed as a lesser creature, and that his life had been cluttered with worry and frustration. But no more. Life was simple now. He fought, mated, swam, ate. He filled his basic needs and desires. Then he slept peacefully, wedged between the fronds of a water plant.

Claire checked on her son hourly. By eight o'clock that evening, Duncan had been sleeping for nine hours straight, and that was after a long sleep the night before. At the office, other parents of teenagers always complained how much their kids slept, but Duncan wasn't usually like that.

"Duncan?"

She brushed the hair off his clammy forehead. Drool bubbled from the side of his mouth. She wiped it away with a tissue and took his temperature again: 95. Subnormal.

"Darling, *please* wake up. . . ."

He was scaring her. She didn't know if she could handle Duncan being sick. Duncan didn't know this, but lately she felt close to slipping over the edge. Work was crazy. Money was tight. She had no close friend to confide in. There was only Duncan. Not that she could confide in him, but at least he was always there, the only reliable constant in her life.

"DUNCAN, *WAKE UP!*"

She slapped his cheek to see if she could raise a response. Sluggishly, he opened his eyes, then his mouth . . . but no words came out. Just bubbling drool. He looked at her as if he didn't know who she was, but he seemed to know the fish. Weakly, he raised his hand and rested it on the side of the vase—*her* vase.

*"Look at ME!"* she shouted, grabbing his face and turning it toward her.

Duncan looked puzzled, then closed his eyes. A sob escaped her tightly closed lips. What a monster she was, yelling at her son when he was sick. She pulled him up and hugged him tight. Duncan's T-shirt was stuck to his back with sweat. He drooled on her neck, fishy-smelling drool. Claire wondered if the salmon loaf had made him sick. *She* felt fine, but. . . .

As she eased Duncan back on the bed, a loud fart ripped out of him and diarrhea oozed onto the sheets. In horror, Claire ran to call for an ambulance.

No one could figure out what was wrong with Duncan, even after they moved him to the Hospital for Sick Children in Toronto and ran every imaginable test. He still had a sub-normal temperature, and loss of bladder and bowel control, but the medical staff could find no physical reason for it. After the first day, his diarrhea cleared up, but he appeared to have no desire to use a toilet or memory of what it was for. He spent the first days in a wheelchair, waving his arms about, but once he tried walking there was no stopping him. Diaper drooping, he paced the hallways, legs jerking, wobbling, and sometimes giving way. He'd pull himself back up again, laughing and smacking his legs as if to say, "Behave!"

Claire told the doctors about the salmon loaf and also Duncan's pet fish in case either thing might be making him sick and causing that unpleasant fishy smell. His tests had come back normal, but Claire still sensed the odor on him. The nurses hinted that Duncan had bigger problems right now than body odor, but to maintain his dignity, Claire bought him deodorant in the hospital's pharmacy, and asked a nurse to help get him into the shower. Duncan loved the shower. He grinned wide, letting the water spray right in his mouth. He waved his arms all around and fought when they tried to take him out.

When he wasn't pacing or in the shower, Duncan sat quietly in bed, pillows propped around him. He stared into space, eyes wide and vacant. He let saliva pool in his mouth and blew bubbles with it, like a baby.

Claire used her vacation time so she could stay near the hospital. At the end of two weeks, she went home to pick up the mail and water the plants. The house smelled stale. Claire ran her fingertips over the rose-colored walls, trying to remember what life had been like before she lost her son. What she wanted to do was crawl into bed and sleep, sleep like Duncan had slept, for a day or more, and wake up to find it had all been a dream. Or she might wake up to find herself drooling and soiling the bed. She'd hardly slept for fear that what happened to Duncan might happen to her too.

She chose efficiency over self-indulgence and dealt with the mail. Bills, a postcard from Randy, and a ton of junk which she tossed in the recycling box. She slipped the postcard into her purse to take to Duncan. The picture on it was crude—a bimbo wearing a thong bikini—but if it would help bring Duncan back, she was willing to try. She watered the downstairs plants, then climbed the stairs to water the fern in her bedroom. As she passed Duncan's door, she suddenly went cold. She had forgotten about feeding the fish.

Claire thought of her self-control as a bridge she constructed every morning out of toothpicks. Right now, her toothpick bridge was swinging in one hell of a wild windstorm . . . *She couldn't remember everything! She couldn't do everything! Hold down a job—keep her and Duncan afloat—and now he was sick—and no one would help—AND HOW WAS SHE SUPPOSED TO REMEMBER TO FEED THE GODDAMNED FISH?*

She threw the watering can against Duncan's door and sank to the floor, sobbing. When the toothpick bridge slowed its swinging, and her breath became regular again, she picked herself up, got a towel from the bathroom, and sopped up the spill. Then, slowly, she walked into Duncan's room.

After a while, the dream changed. The world became smaller, much smaller. The females were gone. The males were gone. The two-legged humans were gone. All that remained was a sunken, shrunken castle with a pathetic little skull and a plant that tasted bad. The water was filthy. There was no food in this place and he was hungry. He nosed around the marbles in the bottom, but all he found was fish turd—his own, he guessed, from the smell. When the hunger got too bad, he tried eating one, but it made him nauseous and he spat it back out. To fill the time, he made a nest, the most magnificent nest yet. Every day, he added to it and rearranged the bubbles. If ever a female came along, he knew she would not be able to resist this nest, which was good because his fins were not the long beauties they had once been.

One day, he heard noises from the world outside the glass. At first they were distant but then—CRASH! That was close. He felt the violent vibrations of it. And then—a human voice, shrieking, sobbing, saying something familiar. *Duncan.* Why did that sound so familiar?

Wendy A. Lewis                                                    143

Across the room, there was movement. A human walked to him and rested her hand on the side of his prison. He flared his gills at her. The woman's face changed, as if the sun had been shining on it, then went behind a cloud. Her hand clenched into a fist. He trembled at the surface. Lack of food was making him weak, confused. It was these close quarters. Not enough room to do things. Too much time to think.

*Mom.* The word filled his mind. *Mom.* He should know what it meant but he'd forgotten. The rule he lived by was: if you don't know what it is, assume it's an enemy. If he had to fight he would. Even if he had to fight a female. Even if he had to fight a human.

It took all of Claire's self-control not to smash her fist against the glass. It wasn't fair. Her son was receiving the best care and attention, yet he wasn't getting better, while this stupid fish was ignored and appeared none the worse, except that his water reeked and there was a horrid foam on the surface.

The compassionate part of her knew that she should change the water and take the fish to Duncan. But a bigger part of her stung from the fact that when the ambulance had come, Duncan had recoiled from her touch and reached for the vase and the fish that had probably caused the whole problem. That smell on Duncan . . . she just *knew* it was the fish's fault. Besides, he was shitting in her vase.

Murk rose from the bottom as she lifted the heavy glass. She gagged all the way to the bathroom and stood in front of the toilet, uncertain what to do. She couldn't dump the fish in without the marbles and plant and castle falling in.

The stupid pretty boy fish was trying to save its life by puffing up and fanning those ridiculously long fins. She screamed at it—no words, just pure, anguished rage—and slammed the vase down on the floor. The skull clinked against the side. Murky water swished onto the gleaming pink tiles. Sobbing again, her breath coming in jerky rasps, she rummaged through the cupboards, searching for rubber gloves. Three tries to get them on. Grimacing, she lowered one gloved hand into the filthy water, pulled out the plant, and dumped it in the garbage. Same thing with the skull and castle. But what, she wondered, could she do with the marbles? She held the vase in one hand and tipped it over the toilet bowl, letting the fish water drain through her fingers and into the toilet.

The fish went wild, fighting gravity and the pull of the water around him. His world shook in the woman's hands. The marbles clinked and rolled against him. His water was disappearing . . . but he'd heard the trickling sound of water falling into water. Maybe this wasn't to be his execution after all! Maybe she was trying to set him free!

He dove . . . and splashed into a bowl that was larger than his former prison, but still it had walls and these ones he could not even see through. He heard a roar, a rushing, and was swept into a whirlpool that sucked him down a dark tunnel with narrow, jagged walls.

His last thought before he gave into the pain was: *Mom*. This time, he remembered who she was. And he remembered who he was—*Duncan*—and where he was supposed to be, but something had gone terribly wrong.

Duncan opened his mouth to scream, but all that came out was a bubble.

The human female, the boy's mother, was back. She had brought him things. A picture of another female. This female was almost naked. She was showing her rump, as if she wanted to mate.

"It's a postcard from Randy," the boy's mother said. "Don't you remember Randy, Duncan?"

Duncan. He remembered Duncan. His friend. His friend whose face he saw when he looked in the shiny glass called . . .

mirror. Yes, mirror. Duncan was in the mirror. Duncan's hands were in his lap. He was learning to walk with Duncan's legs. Walking was fun. Not as fun as swimming but—

"Duncan?"

She always called him that. It must be his new name. First he was Flash. Now he was Duncan.

"Stay with me, Duncan . . . that's better. See the writing on the back? See Randy's name? Do you remember Randy?"

He closed his eyes—it helped to block everything else out. Then he explored the pathways of the boy's brain. Duncan's brain. *His* brain. Using the brain was fun. He discovered new things every day, things he could do, things he could remember . . . Randy. There he was, in the boy's brain. Yellow hair, big smile.

He nodded.

"Oh Duncan! You do? You remember Randy?"

He nodded again and flared his gills. The boy's mother winced. She put her hands on his puffed-out cheeks.

"Please don't do that, Duncan. Thank you. Now, let's put Randy's postcard right here on your table, shall we? How's that?"

The writing faced out. Words were important to humans, he knew, but he hadn't spoken any words yet. That part of his brain was still a jumble. He turned the postcard around so he could see the female who wanted to mate. The boy's mother frowned. Then laughed.

"Okay, okay. Want to see what else I brought? It's what you asked for . . . right before . . . well, here it is."

He raised the pink jug to his lips.

"No! It's not for drinking. Come, I'll show you."

She led him outside. He liked outside. Outside was called . . . the courtyard. It was like a castle, with stone walls and trees.

The boy's mother opened the jug and pulled out a pink wand. She held it to her lips and blew . . . a bubble! A beautiful bubble that lifted on the breeze. He grabbed the wand and blew. Nothing.

"Dip it in the jug, Duncan, like this. Now blow."

Not one bubble came out, but three! Four! Five! He dipped again and blew. Dipped and blew. The sky filled with bubbles. He puffed out his cheeks and waved his arms and laughed. The woman laughed too. But she was also crying. Was she happy or sad?

*Mom.*

A word. One of the words that make humans so happy. He opened his mouth.

"Mmm. . . ." His voice was croaky, unsure. "Mmuuhh. . . ."

"Yes, darling? Yes?"

"Mmuuumm. Mmum!"

"Oh, Duncan!"

She liked his word. Connections started clicking in his brain. Females like words. Females like bubbles. Words are like bubbles! He would make more words and females would love him!

The female—*Mom*—wrapped her fins around him—*Duncan.* He relaxed against her, basking in a moment of pure, uncluttered happiness. It felt so good to be loved, so good to be *alive!*

## X X X X X

*Wendy A. Lewis was born in Ottawa and resides in Uxbridge, Ontario, where her children's menagerie of creepy, crawly pets gives her lots of story ideas. Wendy has been a retail store owner and marketing represen-tative, but now devotes her time to her true love, writ-ing. One of the stories in her first book,* Graveyard Girl, *won the Canadian Authors' Association Vicky Metcalf Award for excellence in young adult short fiction. She is currently working on a second collection of stories for teens which explores the horror and humor of changing bodies, emotions, and relationships.*

# Sweet Sixteen

## Sylvo Frank

*A hhh.* Tim put his feet up by the fire and relaxed. He'd driven over two hours to get to the cottage, and now here he was, finally, all alone, no three older brothers to drive him crazy, no three older sisters to get on his nerves. No, it was just him and the fire, which suited him just fine.

He put another log into the stove and watched it smoke. He loved the heady aroma of burning pine, loved the hissing and spitting of the wood as it burned. He listened to it for a long time.

Outside, November winds howled, sending waves crashing into the shore of the nearby bay. These sounds were like a lull-aby for Tim; he pulled a blanket around himself and snuggled back into the couch, then gazed at the twisting flames until he fell asleep.

He awoke in darkness, just embers glowing in the stove, the skeletal shadows of moonlit trees clawing at the curtains. Sounds had roused him, and now again he heard them: logs cascading down the woodpile by the side of the cottage, and growls. *Damn raccoons.*

Tim needed more wood anyway, so he put on a jacket and went outside. He figured he'd scare off the coon, and get a couple more logs while he was at it.

"Get lost, raccoon. Scram! I'm here, so hit the road."

Tim spoke out loud so as to alert the beast, even though he couldn't see it, couldn't see much of anything really, since clouds had obscured the moon. Logs lay scattered around the wood pile, so Tim picked a few up, grabbed a fistful of kindling, then turned to go back inside, but a sudden whiff of something malodorous cut him short. Had some creature died nearby, leaving a corpse to rot? Tim sniffed the air, trying to locate the source of the foulness, but then the moon burst through, revealing— not ten feet away—a man, standing perfectly still, staring at him.

Tim started at the sight, dropping some of his wood. What was this stranger doing in his yard in the middle of the night? And how long had he been standing there, mute and watching? Wariness crept up Tim's back.

"Can I help you?"

The man smiled, his white teeth gleaming in the moonlight. "Tim," he said, "so nice to see you again."

"Do I know you?"

The man laughed. "No, Tim, *not yet.*"

Coldness in the man's voice made Tim shudder. Maybe the guy had a perfectly good reason for being there; still, Tim'd feel better when he was gone.

"Who are you?"

"*You* may call me Hunter, if you wish."

Hunter. Tim had never heard of him.

Tim glanced up the driveway; but saw only his own car parked there. Clearly Hunter hadn't driven over, yet his clothes—long black overcoat open to the wind, black pants and turtleneck, polished black shoes—just weren't right for a night walk in the country. Besides, Tim knew all their neighbors had already left for the season.

"So, Hunter, what are you doing here? Do you have a flat?" Tim did his best to make his voice sound calm, nonchalant, even though he felt neither, for the man's presence—his uncanny stillness—unnerved him.

Hunter cocked his head. "Why, I've come to invite you to a party."

"I don't want to go to a party."

"Tch, tch. The others will be disappointed."

"What others?"

"Why, my friends, of course. We've been watching you now for a long, long time."

A chill shot up Tim's back. "What are you talking about?"

"Come, I'll introduce you."

"Get the fuck off my property!"

"Language, Tim, not to mention manners."

Hunter stepped towards Tim.

"Stay away from me!" Hunter had no weapon that Tim could see, but he was considerably bigger than Tim. Without taking his eyes off Hunter, Tim edged toward a nearby axe.

Hunter took another step.

Tim flung the rest of his wood in Hunter's direction, then ran for the axe, grabbed it, and brandished it before him. The thought of using it made him nauseous, but he'd use it if he had to.

Hunter laughed. "Surely you weren't wanting to hurt me?"

"Get lost!"

Hunter stopped laughing, stopped smiling. His eyes grew larger, darker, as he fixed Tim in his gaze, and began to walk slowly, deliberately, toward him. Tim backed away, fear and adrenaline coursing through him in equal measure. He couldn't get back inside the cottage without turning his back on Hunter, and even if he could, what then? Call 911? His parents? His absent neighbors? Who could get there before Hunter got in?

"Come," said Hunter, his voice low and hard as he extended a hand towards Tim. Tim swung at it with the axe, a feint meant to put Hunter off-balance just long enough for Tim to rush him, to jab the butt of the axe handle into his gut and his shoulder against Hunter's chest, and thus to send him sprawling, giving himself a chance to hightail it into the surrounding woods, but Hunter merely side-stepped the feint, easily, elegantly, as though he were dancing, then kicked Tim hard in the side, sending him hurtling towards the car.

Tim hit it headfirst, then bounced off it, falling backwards onto the gravel driveway. He groaned as blood trickled from his forehead and the spinning world slowly ground to a halt. The axe lay at his feet and Hunter now knelt beside him; the reek of the man made Tim gag.

Tim glanced at Hunter's eyes, but the man didn't look back; he seemed transfixed by the bleeding gash over Tim's left eyebrow. Hunter stroked the wound with icy fingers, then began to probe it. Tim winced. Hunter then brought his bloodied fingers to his nose, closed his eyes, and sniffed the blood, breathing long and slow, smiling all the while. Instinctively, Tim pulled away. Hunter opened his eyes and looked at Tim. "You really must come to the party."

Tim wondered what kind of freak he was dealing with, but said nothing. Hunter then grabbed a fistful of Tim's jacket, pulled him up so that they were face to face, and said, "Really, I insist."

In a single fluid motion, Hunter stood up, dragging Tim up with him. He flung Tim over his shoulder, then began to run towards the forest.

Although shocked by Hunter's strength, Tim struggled anyway, pounding on Hunter's back with his fists while trying to kick his legs free. He soon realized this was pointless though, as

Hunter maintained an unwavering canter regardless. Helpless, Tim watched Hunter's coat tails flap before his eyes, watched dirt and stone and rotting leaves fly by, felt the painful throbbing of blood in his head. Beneath him, the easy gait of muscle and bone seemingly oblivious to its burden, like that of a wolf returning home with its kill.

Tim prayed he was merely in the throes of a nightmare, but he knew, his body knew, it wasn't so.

The forest floor gave way to a clearing of frostbitten grass; at its center Hunter stopped, then dumped Tim at his feet.

"We're here, Tim. Having fun yet?" Hunter smiled, then leaned his head back and howled. The sound of it, so visceral, so intense, so unnervingly canine, left Tim wondering if the man was even human at all.

In the distance, another howl echoed the first, then another, long and low.

"If you really want to go, Tim, now's your chance." Once again, Hunter stood perfectly still.

Tim forced himself up to his feet, despite his pain and dizziness, and hobbled towards the woods as fast as he could. Once, he turned to see if Hunter pursued him, but no, not yet.

Then, just as he was about to reach the woods' edge, he saw a woman with long blonde hair, dressed in black, blocking his path. Tim looked at her, and the shiver of ice that cut through him told him to go another way. He turned to his right, but there too, he saw someone, a young man now, barely older than himself, also dressed in black and smiling, ambling towards him. He turned to the left; two women there, dark hair blowing in the wind. The shorter one licked her lips as she stared at him.

"No," he shouted, "leave me alone!" But no one paid any attention to his words as the ring encircling him grew tighter.

"Monsters! You're all fucking monsters!" Tears rolled down Tim's face as he picked up a rock and threw it at one of circle.

He missed. "Fuck you!" he screamed. He threw another, missed again. Now he was out of rocks.

The ring closed in. Finally, Hunter walked up to him, put a finger on Tim's lips and said, "Time for you to be quiet."

"No!" said Tim, but Hunter opened his hand, covering Tim's mouth, and pushed him backwards, sending him sprawling onto the ground. The others swooped down upon him. He felt their icy hands upon his body as they lifted him up, entwining him in their arms, felt their putrid breath upon his skin, felt his own warmth, the beating of his heart, the soaring of it, the liquid life pumping through him and then the bites piercing his neck, his wrists, his thighs. He could feel *them* sucking and himself getting colder, cold as the moon, his head swinging, his body swimming, rocking like the bony trees cavorting overhead.

Sunlight on his eyelids woke him up. Opening them, he saw a rectangle of blue sky framed by dark walls of earth. He flexed his fingers, felt soil below, then sat up, the effort taxing his hurt, shivering body. He remembered the night before, the vampires drinking—for what else could they have been? He'd seen the movies, had read the books and had enjoyed them, but never had believed them until now. He touched the twin holes on his wrists and neck; like dark stigmata they were, raw, red proof of evil. Yet here he was, alive sort of—at least he thought he was alive. The sunlight didn't hurt, although everything else did.

Help. He needed help, but where to get it? And how? He didn't even know where he was, nor did he have any idea where the beasts had gone, but if they were really vampires, then surely they couldn't be out now? Be awake? So why had they left him here, so weak, but still breathing? Were they toying with him? Or had they left him alive for some other purpose?

He didn't want to know. Mostly he just wanted to get out of the hole, so like a grave, and then it struck him that maybe it was *his* grave they were digging. This thought gave him the dry heaves.

After he regained his composure, Tim listened for any sounds above that might indicate where he was, or who—if anyone—was there. He heard nothing, just the wind, so he gathered his strength, then stood up and peeked out of the grave. To his surprise, he found himself alone in the middle of the clearing where Hunter had deposited him the night before. Beside his grave stood a large mound of dirt and an open coffin, fresh hewn. He climbed out of the grave, then inched toward the coffin and cautiously peered inside. Empty. He breathed a sigh of relief.

The coffin's lid lay on the ground a few feet away. It bore an inscription, but dirt covered most of the letters. Tim crawled over and began to wipe away the dirt. Gradually, a name appeared, *his* name: Timothy Henry Fitzpatrick.

Tim stared aghast at the roughly chiseled letters, and read his name over and over. He was in danger of succumbing to despair; if he ever hoped to escape, he had to do so now. He stood up and tried to get his bearings.

The sun hung low in the sky. Was it morning? Evening? He couldn't tell nor did the clearing look familiar even in the light of day. Then he scanned the horizon hoping for a clue, and got one: off in the distance, Smoke Mountain. Now he knew where he was, more or less, and knew that he couldn't be more than a few miles from the cottage. But could he make it back before dark? Or at least to Concession Road 14? There he might be able to flag someone down, get a lift to the hospital or the police or maybe even a church—anywhere away from here. He turned in the direction of the mountain, and began to walk.

Every step hurt, but he kept on, out of the clearing and into the forest, doing his best to keep on course. His body cried for rest, but he knew that would mean certain death, or even worse, undeath, although the legends weren't consistent on that score. Did he have to drink the blood of a vampire to become one himself? And had he? He couldn't remember.

Waning light informed him that the day was ending, not beginning; he could feel the darkness rising along with his panic. He redoubled his efforts, then just as the sun kissed the horizon, he reached the concession road.

He stood by its side and prayed for a car to appear. Minutes later a red pick-up truck pulled into view, but to Tim's dismay it sped past, despite his frantic waving, with nary a glance from the driver. Meanwhile another truck had zoomed by in the other direction; Tim hobbled over to the middle of the road and waved both arms at its disappearing bulk, willing its driver to catch sight of him in his rearview mirror and stop, but the vehicle continued to speed away, its tail lights vanishing in the blood-red twilight.

Tim sighed, exhausted. He returned to the road's edge, then dropped to his knees and waited, trying to quell his fear. Nearby, an owl hooted, once, twice, its cry lingering in the creeping silence. A minute later, the blessed sound of an engine approaching. Tim no longer had the strength to stand up, so he crawled as close to the road as he dared, then waved at the oncoming SUV. The glare of its headlights blinded him, but he pumped an arm regardless; to his relief, the vehicle stopped.

A woman got out and rushed to his side. "Timmy, what's wrong? What happened?" Tim could've kissed Mrs. Fausz.

"Please, help me," he said. "Get me out of here, fast."

"Can you stand up?"

"Can you help me up?"

Mrs. Fausz positioned herself by Tim's side and grabbed him under the armpits. "Okay," she said, "on the count of three: one, two—"

A sharp crack interrupted the woman's words. She fell to the ground beside Tim and lay there motionless, her head twisted into an unnatural position.

"Mrs. Fausz?" Tim touched her arm, but she said nothing. Then he smelled it, the now-familiar stench of the undead. He turned around and saw Hunter standing behind him, stretching his arms. Hunter cracked his knuckles.

"I love twilight, don't you, Tim?"

Tim closed his eyes, and felt his hopes sink along with the sun.

"Surely you weren't thinking to leave so soon?" The vampire chuckled, then took hold of Tim's right arm and dragged him over Mrs. Fausz's still-warm body, across the road, and back into the forest. Tim barely even registered the pain of it.

The vampire hummed as he walked.

"Didn't you enjoy your birthday party? Sweet sixteen, is it not? Certainly my companions did. Sweet, yes that's what they said, *That Tim, he's so sweet. And salty too, just how we like them.* True, we were a few months late for the celebration, but better late than never, no?"

The vampire stopped abruptly, letting go of Tim's arm. "Oh, my manners—I forgot to invite your friend! But none of us like O positive, I'm afraid. Too pedestrian. And even if we did, she'd be cold by the time we got back, and *nobody* likes them cold." Hunter bent down, jabbed his face into Tim's, then turned Tim's chin to face his own. "So sorry."

Tim tried to spit in Hunter's face but managed only to dribble onto his own chin.

Hunter laughed. "Oh, what a spunky lad we have here. An excellent choice."

He stood up, then continued on through the woods, dragging Tim behind him, until, once again, they were back in the clearing.

The other vampires stood around the coffin, waiting.

"What would you like first, Tim, a drink or your present? Hmm? Can't decide?"

The vampires laughed at this, but Tim refused to answer; his loathing for the creatures keeping his jaws shut.

Hunter pulled Tim up to his knees. "Very well, then, I'll choose for you. Let's see . . . I choose . . . the gift. Ta-da!"

Hunter swept his hand before the coffin. "We made it especially for you. Do you like it?"

Before Tim could answer the question, though, Hunter picked him up. "Here, Nora, catch!" He hurled Tim to the blonde vampire. To Tim's horror, she not only caught him, but tossed him to another, who tossed him to yet another, who bobbed him back to Nora as though he were nothing more than a kitty toy.

They all had Hunter's freakish strength.

"Seamus, catch!"

The vampires threw Tim back and forth over the open coffin, then stuffed him into it. He tried to climb back out, but every time he lifted a limb, a vampire would playfully push it back inside.

"Enough!" said Hunter. The others stepped away from the coffin. Tim tried to sit up, but now Hunter pushed him back down, then said, "Here's a sneak preview of coming attractions."

Peals of laughter met Tim's ears as the coffin lid slipped into place above him, encasing him in darkness.

"No!" Tim screamed as he heard the nails get hammered in. Every blow reverberated through the wood and into his own body. In time, the hammering stopped; so did his screaming.

"Tim, can you hear me?"

"Let me out!"

"You can? Good. Are you thirsty?"

"Let me out!"

"Just one little drink, Tim, and the freedom of the night will be yours, the glory of the darkness. All you have to do is ask."

"Let me out!"

"Tch tch tch. I'm afraid this won't do. You simply have to play by the rules. Think about it."

Before Tim could say a word, he felt the coffin lift up, with him inside it. His weight shifted back and forth as the coffin tilted, lowered, then came to rest. And then the muffled sound of something hitting the coffin over and over while the vampires cackled. As the sounds got dimmer, a realization crept over Tim: he was being buried alive.

He screamed and screamed again, unable to move, unable to turn, unable to do anything more than wiggle his toes or his fingers, or turn his head. The rancid smell of his own fear engulfed him, followed by the acid tinge of his own shit when he lost control of his bowels.

He wondered how long his air would last, and what his parents were doing, and who would miss him first. Would they come for him? Would they call? Had they already?

The sound of digging caught Tim's attention. It grew louder, closer, and then a scraping on the coffin itself, followed by silence.

Three knocks on the coffin's lid.

"Hello! Anybody in?" Hunter's voice.

Laughter and then the screech of splintering wood as the coffin's lid came off, allowing Tim fresh air and a view of the starry sky, as well as of Hunter and the others.

"Ugh!" said Seamus, "what a stench."

"Yes, the reek of mortality."

Hunter looked Tim in the eye. "So, my little wonder, come to any decision?" Tim ignored him, focusing on Orion in the sky above.

"I see. Very well, then. Nora, perhaps you might persuade him?"

"Not smelling like that!"

"Well, then, wash him!"

Nora grumbled as she pulled Tim out of the coffin, then dragged him along behind her. Soon Tim could hear the crashing of waves; the sound grew until he found himself looking out over the churning lake.

Nora flung him into the water; its icy coldness took his breath away. He hoped he'd drown, that the waves would spare him an unnatural death, but Nora waded in after him and grasped him firmly by the collar. She dragged him to and fro through the water, then pulled him back onto the beach. He lay there shivering, and coughing up water until his lungs cleared. His shivering though, didn't cease, nor had he the strength to stand up, so he remained face down in the sand, his head turned to one side.

"He's dying, Hunter."

"Yes." Hunter lay down beside Tim, bit his own finger until it bled, then let the dark liquid drip inches from Tim's face. "This is it, Tim—live forever . . . or not."

Tim watched the blood drip, each gleaming drop twisting in the moonlight. He wanted to live, but not like this, not like them. He closed his eyes and pulled his head away from Hunter's blood, resolution settling in his bones.

Hunter sighed. "I had such hopes for you, seventh child of a seventh child and all. You were made for this life, but no matter. I'll find another."

Someone caressed his cheek, his lips, his throat, but Tim barely noticed. Then once again Hunter spoke: "*He's yours.*"

A howling, the swish of garments, and the dull pain of teeth stabbing into him, the noisy, hungry sucking, and *their* odor, so foul mixing with the sweet scent of the lake, and the cries of the water as it lashed the shore, and the wind, always the wind, moaning, then fading into the distance, fading away into the silent dark.

# X X X X X

*Although a Winnipegger by birth, Sylvo Frank has lived most of his life in Toronto, where he is currently a child care worker. Sylvo has had two other stories published: "Graveyard Studies" appeared in the anthology* The Horrors I *(Red Deer Press: 2005).* "The Fox and the Wolf" *appeared in the anthology* At the Edge: A Book of Risky Stories.

# FINGERS

## Alison Lohans

The *Taku Spirit* loomed huge, white, with rows of portholes peppering its massive sides. Bright flags fluttered from one of the top decks; seagulls screeched overhead in the Vancouver sunshine. Excitement leapt in Austin's gut as he stared at the ship. It seemed impossible that in a few minutes he'd be on board.

Along with his relatives—Uncle James and Aunt Angelica, and his cousin Riley. The last time he'd seen them was for Grandpa's funeral. Austin's neck tightened at a rush of memories. Johnnie Walker bottles lying around for Mom to clean up. And the yelling . . . There'd been a scary fight, with Aunt Angelica and Uncle James screaming at Dad for something Austin didn't understand, and that nobody would explain later. Aunt Angelica hadn't seemed very sad about Grandpa.

Standing with them now in the lineup, Austin could think of better company for a seven-day Alaska cruise. But Uncle James and Aunt Angelica had insisted that he come, and even paid his way. A peace offering, Dad said. Besides, it would be a change from spending the whole summer with his parents at the cottage on Lake of Bays, in Muskoka.

Riley was pacing restlessly. He had a hulking presence, almost gorilla-like. Austin didn't know him very well; they'd only seen each other four or five times, even though they were the same age. There was a tension between the two families that dated back to some kind of gruesome accident when Dad was a kid. Now, Riley caught his glance and reciprocated with a smirk. As if he knew something that Austin didn't.

"Well, here we are."

Austin winced at Uncle James' jovial statement of the obvious. An instant later he stepped on his own dangling shoelace; he lurched off balance and his backpack whacked Aunt Angelica's shoulder. Her hiss of annoyance brought a wash of heat to his cheeks. "I'm sorry," he stammered. His aunt ignored his apology.

"Welcome to the *Taku Spirit*. Please step over here. . . ." A photographer ushered them to a panel showing mountains and a glacier. Austin froze in position, feeling Uncle James' beefy hand clamp around his shoulder, the tickle of his uncle's boozy breath against his neck. A quick flash; then they were on the gangway leading into the ship.

Dazzling glitter. Refracted light from crystal chandeliers, mirrors, the gold gleam of railings. A string quartet was playing. White-gloved, uniformed crew greeted travelers with handshakes and smiles. A red-coated steward met Uncle James and Aunt Angelica; another one approached Austin. "I am. . . ." He uttered a multi-syllabled name Austin had never heard before. "I am your cabin steward, and will now take you to your stateroom." His accent was strong, hard to understand.

Austin smiled at him, then instantly felt like a fool. The steward's lips stretched widely around white, polished teeth—

but the man was looking at Aunt Angelica, who responded with a curt nod. Might as well be a suitcase, for all this guy seemed to care! He led them to an elevator and down to the Orca deck, the lowest level of the ship, and then along a seemingly endless corridor of closed doors. Finally he unlocked room 728. Riley pushed in first. "I get the bed with the TV," he said.

The cabin was small and cramped. Two twin beds occupied most of the space; squeezed in nearer to the door were a small couch, a chair, and a table. Austin sagged onto his bed. He'd been up since 3 a.m. eastern time to catch the flight from Pearson, so it had already been a long day.

After the lifeboat drill, Austin went to the captain's departure party on the Chilkoot deck. As he and Riley stood there chewing meaty slices of pizza, the *Taku Spirit* shuddered. A deep-voiced horn blasted. Imperceptibly at first, the surroundings shifted sideways—a log barge, a float plane *putting* along the greeny-brown surface, Canada Place. . . . They were on their way.

Austin raced up two flights of steps to the Aurora deck. "This is *cool!*" he said to Riley, who'd followed reluctantly.

"I guess." Riley clicked a control on his Discman.

Austin stared in awe at white-peaked mountains, at the Lion's Gate Bridge arching across the water. Another prolonged bellow from the horn; they glided beneath the bridge with its scuttling traffic, then, decisively, left it behind.

"I'm going to the internet café." Riley walked off, slouched as usual.

While excited tourists snapped photos and gazed through binoculars, Austin leaned over the rail. Far below, a miniature tugboat trailed a plume of exhaust; an even tinier sailboat cautiously skirted the two bigger vessels. How long would it take to hit the water if he fell? He studied a life preserver roped to a boxy wooden bench that supposedly contained forty life jackets.

This boat was a fancy hotel, heading out to sea—unreal, compared to the Ontario cottage that had been in the family for a hundred years. If he were there, he could be clearing up debris washed up onto the beach—or helping Dad with the outhouse. Or kayaking. . . . Were the Morrises there yet? Last year Cherelle had morphed from a chunky, freckle-faced brat into a shapely, freckle-faced girl who occasionally blushed when she looked at him. Instead of pushing each other off the raft or, on rainy days, clobbering each other at Monopoly, they'd been oddly shy. At night, he'd lain awake in his bed on the screened porch, thinking about things that used to seem gross, but now were . . . tantalizing.

The *Taku Spirit* picked up speed. Ahead, Austin could see the dark humps of the Gulf Islands. Probably Vancouver Island too, that bluish mountain range in the distance. The wind jiggled his shirt sleeves, puckered the skin on his arms.

He went inside. The gym was on the Chilkoot deck. Nearby, people were eating at a buffet. He checked out the spread and grabbed a handful of grapes. Wandering down to the Tlingit level, he found an awesome carved totem pole and the ship's stores, filled with jewelry and clothing and souvenirs. In the casino, Uncle James was sitting at a table with several stacks of chips laid out before him on the green felt. Lingering, Austin saw the dealer scoop up those chips, *all* of them, saw his uncle sigh and gulp his drink, and then set out three more stacks. Austin turned away, feeling sick. His relatives were pretty rich, but still. . . . An elevator took him down to the Orca level. Many of the people in the corridors were speaking other languages. The whine of a vacuum cleaner cut through their voices.

It was the cabin steward with the robot smile. Austin hurried past to 728 and slid his ID card into the lock. The little light spurted red, not green. He tried again; same thing. Reluctantly, he approached the steward. "I can't unlock my door," he said.

Was the guy deaf? He kept right on vacuuming. The immaculate red jacket swished faintly as its owner glided the nozzle across the floor.

Austin cleared his throat. "Excuse me. . . ."

The man unplugged the vacuum cleaner, tucked the bulky, sinuous hose beneath his arm, and walked away. The dangling cord left a faint trail in the luxuriant, blue-violet carpet.

What was with that arrogant—? Again he tried the key, wrestled with the handle.

"Are you locked out, dear?" A tiny woman approached. Old and wrinkly, with copper-dyed hair, she wore gold necklaces draped over her skimpy chest.

"Uh, yeah. . . ."

"Go to the front desk." Her alert eyes scanned the hallway. "Don't waste your time on that useless steward."

It was so unexpected that Austin almost laughed. "Thanks."

"Is this your first cruise? You'll love it," she continued at his nod. "I've done fifty, and every one's been worth it. My name's Clara Thompson, by the way, and I'm in 731." The woman walked briskly toward a stairway.

Austin went the opposite direction. After a long wait in a line of people signing up for shore excursions, the desk clerk listened to his plight. "This card is defective," she said with apparent surprise; "I'll get you another one." And that was all there was to it.

Many hours later, after the mainland fjords had dissolved into dusky shadows, after a boring meal with his relatives in the formal dining room, after the lights of Campbell River had been left behind and the teen get-together and movie were history, Austin felt uneasy. He and Riley were actually in the cabin at the same time, he with an overloaded bowl of ice cream from the midnight dessert buffet, and Riley with a silver platter of sandwiches from room service. The bed covers had been folded back, and a square of chocolate placed on each pillow. The steward had done this, had even removed the backpack Austin left on his bed. It felt wrong, his personal stuff being handled by a stranger. As he reached for the chocolate, his ice cream overturned onto the clean sheets. Austin swore and scooped it up with the bowl.

"You got a problem?" Riley let out a loud, raunchy fart.

Austin groaned and stepped into the cramped washroom for a towel to clean up the mess. A lumpy object lay in the sink. He glanced at it as he reached for a hand towel, then looked again. It was a finger.

Was this one of Riley's sick pranks? Grabbing his cousin's toothbrush, he gave the finger a nudge. A white knuckle joint glistened within a ring of ragged, bloodless flesh. Sweat beaded Austin's face and neck. He retched, barely making it to the toilet.

Snickering came from the other room. "You seasick already? Shut the door, at least." On TV, the sounds of a gunfight boomed out.

Austin spat, spat again. Gasping, he leaned against the cold toilet bowl. "Nice joke, Riley," he said. "What else've you got planned?"

Instead of answering, his cousin left the cabin.

Now what? He couldn't stay with that . . . thing . . . in the sink. Shakily he stood up. Poked at the finger until it turned over. With its large knuckle and broad nail, it was a man's, probably. Where had it come from? Who did it belong to? Was it even real? Chewing his lip, he touched it. And slumped to sit on the floor while his stomach roiled. Cold flesh somewhat pliant, the nail decidedly hard with little ridges. . . . Something told him this was no fake.

Breathing fast, he leaned against the wall. And saw smeary writing on the mirror.

*This finger points*
*At one who should know*
*All is not well*
*With the status quo.*

Riley would never say something like that. Had he even seen it? What was this supposed to *mean?*

Austin considered calling the front desk—but to tell them what? Uncle James and Aunt Angelica never gave him their stateroom number. He grabbed a towel and scrubbed the mirror. The little squealy sounds shivered his teeth. Numbly he scooped the finger into the towel, wrapped it, and stepped into the hallway. The door banged shut. In his mind's eye, he saw his ship ID on the bedside table. Not again!

He tucked the towel against his hip and caught the elevator, punched *C* for the Chilkoot deck; he could ditch the finger in a garbage can by the swimming pool. The elevator doors yawned open at every floor. Nobody got in—not until a red-jacketed figure joined him at the Bering level. Austin turned to face the mirrored panel. Saw reflected eyes scrutinizing him. The man's lips stretched in a hideous approximation of a smile.

Austin's mouth went dry. Why was the steward watching him like that? He clamped his arm tighter around the towel and jabbed the button for the Yakutat level. The door did not open, didn't open at the Chilkoot deck either. With a whoosh they rose to the Raven deck. The bell dinged; Austin stumbled out of the oppressive cage. For a moment he thought about running across the tennis court to throw the thing over the side of the ship, then changed his mind. It was too dark out there.

Few people were around—except for an unhurried tread following him whichever way he turned. One of the steward's shoes made a soft *scrunch* with every footfall. Down the elegant staircase. On the Chilkoot deck, a lone pipe smoker lounged beside the pool. That meant two witnesses if he dumped it in the garbage.

Down to Tlingit level. The steward was still tailing him. What if the finger fell out of the towel? Past the casino, with its lights and clanging bells. Strains of music led him to the piano bar, where a hot blonde was singing. Uncle James and Aunt Angelica were there, into the booze as usual. Austin claimed a low-profile corner spot, stuffing his bundle behind the chair. Later, he could just walk away. His hands felt grotesquely filthy. He studied them—ten fingers, all intact. Whose finger was in the towel? Out of the corner of his eye, he could see the steward lurking by a ceramic urn. Aunt Angelica was looking that direction, too. A moment later, the steward was gone.

The day had been completely disjointed; now, everything faded into a blur. His parents seeing him off at the security gate, all smiles and hugs. The long wait, then the flight. His parents would be back in Muskoka. That was one thing about the cottage—it was peaceful there. With a jolt, he remembered the freaky moment in the limo on the way to Canada Place: Aunt Angelica, with her champagne glass poised. Her lipsticked mouth compressed into prune mode as her green eyes bored into him, while a gold-sandalled foot tapped restlessly. He shuddered. What was *that* about? He wished he had his cell phone, hoped it was still in his backpack. A friendly voice would be great, just now. At home, it was almost five a.m.

He drifted. Piano notes and singing tangled with his thoughts.

He dreamed about the cottage. There was a new white sign nailed to the birch tree by the front door: *Loon's Landing, Lake of Bays—Eternal property of the oldest son. Michael Weekes, father of Austin Weekes.* Then he was on horseback, cantering along a forested trail. "*Pssst!*" A voice in his ear. Nobody was there, just him and the horse, and some chickadees busy in the trees. Something about Uncle James and Aunt Angelica and Riley coming—except, that couldn't be right. Rich Albertans *never* came to Loon's Landing. The horse ran faster.

"*Pssst!* Wake up!"

His back and neck felt crunched. The rocking motion continued. He was in a chair, and an old lady was talking to him. He couldn't remember who she was. Gray, misty light came through huge windows.

The ship. He was on his way to Alaska.

"Wait." She put a restraining hand on his arm. "Our cabin steward was watching you. Gives me the willies, that one."

Adrenaline jolted him fully awake. Should he tell *her* about the finger? He checked behind the chair. No white towel was jammed in there. Sleep-deprived for several nights, maybe his imagination was working overtime? When he stood up, the floor tilted. After a surprised second his knees adapted to the ship's movement. "Thanks, Mrs. . . ."

"Thompson," she supplied with a smile. "Clara. I'll walk back with you; I was out for my morning rounds and wasn't sure I liked what I was seeing here."

Goosebumps rippled up his arms. What had she seen?

The ship wallowed. Earlier, he hadn't noticed the rails lining the hallways; now he grabbed one for support. Mrs. Thompson was amazingly spry in her no-nonsense running shoes. A blue-jacketed room service waiter passed them. As the ship took another plunge, his tray tipped. Plate covers, coffee, cutlery; they all clattered to the floor; somebody's eggs Benedict sat there, surprised, on the carpet. The waiter bent over the mess, muttering in another language. He had a Band-Aid on his left thumb.

"Let me help," Mrs. Thompson said, kneeling beside him.

Austin hesitated, then kept going. Beyond the ship's library was a wall map with a trail of lights indicating their course. A blinking orange dot showed them nearing the Queen Charlotte Islands. On impulse, he went down to the Ketchikan deck, where he pushed through heavy swinging doors and was immersed in the roar of crashing waves. A few hardy walkers were out doing rounds of the deck; he waited for a track-suited man to pass, then leaned against the rail. Water sloshed, sucked, slapped, endless movement. The wind hurled cold rain and spray in his face; the air was sweet and invigorating. No islands in sight—no land, not anywhere. Crew members huddled in one of the doorways, looking half-frozen. Austin glanced at his bare arms and felt himself smile—this was nothing compared to a Canadian winter.

The stern offered shelter from the elements. He stared, mesmerized, at the green-white water churning out from the propeller, a foam-rippled signature in the gray, choppy sea. After a while the bite of cigarette smoke announced company. A man in a black leather jacket was drawing deeply, then spinning out sharp, focused gusts. Impassive eyes surveyed him. The steward. He gestured with his cigarette in a way that was somehow menacing.

Fear sent Austin careening across the wet deck. Downstairs, down corridors of closed doors, lurching by elderly people and little kids as the ship heaved and rolled. At last he found it, 728. He banged with cold fists on the door. "Riley! Let me in!"

It took an eternity for the latch to open. Riley's face was greenish and the acrid odor of puke fouled the cabin air. *Took you long enough.* Austin bit back the remark. His bowl of melted ice cream sat in a sticky puddle on the bedside table. But not his ID card. He dug through the drawers, crawled on hands and knees checking every possible crevice. "Hey, Riley—did you happen to see where my ID card went?"

"I haven't touched your friggin' card." Riley yanked the pillow over his head and lay there, an inert lump.

His backpack? His suitcase? Austin dug through them. No card. Had the steward taken it while Riley was sleeping? Heart slamming against his ribs, he turned on his cell phone. Dialed the cottage in far-away Muskoka. A monotonous bleeping filled his ear. Out of range. Now what? He hit *Power* on the TV remote, and was grateful for the wash of noise. Food would help. He called room service, then the front desk. "My ID card is missing," he said.

"Mr. Riley Hastings?" the receptionist enquired.

"No. Austin Weekes." He could hear computer keys clicking. "Room 728."

"We'll issue you another card, Mr. Wilkes. Bring your passport for confirmation."

*Wilkes?* Most of the crew seemed to be from other countries—but would a foreign accent warp his name that badly? Maybe when his food arrived Riley would be over his seasickness, maybe even go with him to the front desk. E-mail. He could use the internet café. His parents didn't have access at Loon's Landing, but he could get in touch with Cherelle Morris, ask her to talk to Mom or Dad.

He waited. The ship rocked, making him feel slightly queasy. Room service was taking forever. Finally, a tap on the door; a blue-clad waiter set a tray on the table. Austin's mouth watered at the tantalizing smell of bacon. And coffee; at home, his parents didn't let him have it often. He sat on the small couch and lifted the lid. Breakfast! Bacon and two eggs over easy. Toast and hash browns.

And a finger, served with a parsley garnish. This one was smaller and had pale pink polish on the oval nail.

Austin's stomach twisted. Who was doing this? *Why?* He held the door open with one foot, looked up and down the hallway. The waiter was gone. "*Riley!*" He jabbed his cousin until a sullen face confronted him. "Call your parents! There's *another* finger." His eyes went watery as he realized Riley might not know about the first one. Or the weird poem on the mirror.

"Wha—?"

"*Please!* They never gave me their number. Look." He set the tray on Riley's bed. His cousin took one look and spewed all over the breakfast. Holding his breath, Austin set the mess in the hall.

"What kind of sicko would do that?" Riley gasped.

So it wasn't Riley. He watched his cousin punch numbers into the bedside phone. "Dad—somebody put a chopped-off finger in Austin's breakfast!" Riley listened, argued, then banged the receiver down. "He doesn't believe me," he said. "And Mom's in the shower."

There was a knock on the door. Riley yanked the covers over his boxers and bare chest. "You get it."

Another staccato rap. "It's only me."

Austin opened the door for Mrs. Thompson. "That steward is doing his rounds," she whispered. "In case you wanted to know." She looked at the tray on the hall floor. "Oh dear. They have something for seasickness at the front desk."

Would she notice . . . ?

She did. "Oh my Lord!" Muttering about finding the captain, she hurried away.

"Who was that?" Riley asked suspiciously.

"Just this old lady down the hall." Hopefully she *would* tell the captain. Now Austin could hear the sinister whine of the vacuum cleaner. Rummaging through his suitcase, he grabbed a change of underwear. Clean socks, clean shirt, antiperspirant. Toothbrush, toothpaste. He opened the closet safe and got his passport, stuffed everything in his backpack along with his useless cell phone.

When he left, the disgusting breakfast tray had been removed. He found the java bar and grabbed a cup of coffee.

Hot, strong, it cleared his brain. At the internet café he claimed an empty station and typed his way to the log-in page, supplied the needed information. Entered *FINGERS* for a password. Pushed *Submit*. The computer let out a warning *chonkk! ACCESS DENIED*, in flashing red. *PASSENGER NOT ON RECORD*.

*What?!* Austin stared at the screen, his hand clamped on the mouse. There'd been that confusion with the desk clerk; maybe they had him listed as Wilkes. He hadn't really looked at his second ID card. He tried again. No luck. Was it just an error? Or . . . was somebody maybe trying to get rid of him? His neck prickled.

He found a wall phone. Dialed 728. After four long rings his cousin's grumpy voice answered. "Hey, Riley. I can't get online. What do you do?"

Riley's sigh exploded in his ear. "Follow the instructions, idiot." The line clicked.

"Right," he muttered to the dead receiver. Now all the computer stations were in use. On the Chilkoot deck he played ping-pong with a kid from Brazil. Had a burger and fries at the pool-side grill. No spare fingers *there*. He went by the casino. Uncle James was parked at the craps table—losing again, from the looks of it. He went up to the Crow's Nest and played team trivia with a family from Idaho. A cheerful, casual family, who didn't know many of the answers.

Time crawled. The internet café remained busy. He signed up for a whale watching tour in Juneau, and in Skagway, a horseback riding expedition in the Yukon. Would he even be able to get off the boat without his ID? Once again he returned to the front desk.

"We have nobody on record by that name." The clerk flipped through a stack of papers, clearly wanting him gone. Her red fingernails looked dangerous.

"But—!" Austin showed his passport. "I'm traveling with my relatives—James and Angelica Hastings. And their son Riley. We're in room 728."

Blue eyes skewered him. "That room is listed as a single, sir." She picked up a phone. "Security, this is the front desk. We have an unauthorized person on board."

Austin's scalp shrank. He pushed past a burly man who'd stepped up to the counter and was peeling bills from a fat wallet. If he moved in a hurry, he'd draw attention to himself. So he walked aimlessly. Every way he turned, it seemed a red-jacketed figure was disappearing around a corner. And now security, too! Should he call his parents? Except . . . the front desk was playing games with his name. Whoever was behind this could make sure he wouldn't get through. Pretend he was Riley? Even if it worked, he had a horrible feeling Mom and Dad wouldn't be able to do a thing, back in Ontario.

Eventually he returned to 728, the only place he could possibly relax, maybe figure out a plan. "I don't even *want* the friggin' thing." Riley's voice came through the door, in a major sulk. Obviously he had company.

Austin took a zigzag path to the gym and sighed with relief. It was just ordinary people, working the machines. He settled on an exercise bike and pumped hard. Outside, a shadowy island came into view through the rain and clouds. Weights clanged; the smell of sweat hung in the air. One machine after the other, he did determined battle. After a while he was too tired to continue. In the change room, he unzipped his backpack and reached for his clean clothes. A paper crackled—one he hadn't put there himself. He repressed a shudder as he pulled it out. Another poem:

> *This finger points*
> *At one who should know*

*A dire fate awaits,*
*The die cast long ago.*

Invading his backpack! How the hell had that happened? Somebody must've snuck up on him when he was busy with the machines—or maybe waiting in line somewhere? At the internet café? Frantically he hauled things out. Antiperspirant, cell phone, clothes, and all the rest, everything scattered in a tangle on the floor. An older man gave him a curious glance as he proceeded to the shower. Digging through his stuff, Austin's hand settled on a little leather pouch, held shut by a drawstring. Didn't take much guessing to figure out what *that* contained . . .

*Dire fate* . . . He began shaking deep inside and couldn't stop. Had there been a poem with the breakfast finger, too? If so, what did it say? People went by in a haze. And then he remembered Mrs. Thompson. Had she told the captain? Austin shoved the little bag and everything else into his backpack. In the elevator down to Orca level, he was aware of his sweat, and its stink. Of his heart, drumming fast and hard.

Mrs. Thompson's cabin was close to 728, just down the hall. The door was ajar. He knocked. No answer. A red-jacketed figure came out of a stateroom near the elevator. Austin ducked inside; the lock clicked. "Mrs. Thompson?" he whispered. It was weird that she'd leave the door open.

Nobody was there, and he was exhausted. She wouldn't mind if he rested a bit on the couch. His tired eyes saw photos of kids on the desk. A card that said *HAPPY BIRTHDAY, GRANDMA!*

There was a heavy thud. A frisson of terror pierced him. The sound came again. The closet? Shaking, Austin unlatched the hinged door.

The little woman looked up at him with terrified eyes. Her mouth was duct-taped shut; her arms were bound to her sides. A dark bruise mottled her forehead.

Alison Lohans

Austin lifted Mrs. Thompson and set her on the couch. When she jerked her head sideways, he understood. In the washroom he found a pair of tiny scissors. Gingerly, he went to work on the duct tape.

"He's going to throw me overboard!" she gasped as soon as her mouth was clear.

Austin didn't need to ask who. "Let's go to the infirmary," he said. "You'll be safe there." Mrs. Thompson nodded and stumbled along beside him, all the while muttering about being a terrible nuisance, and when would that silly captain put a stop to this nonsense.

The infirmary staff seemed kind, and efficient. "Here," Mrs. Thompson said as Austin turned to leave. "You may need this." She thrust her ID card into his hand.

In room 731, Austin checked his backpack. The contents seemed intact—including the pouch. By the feel of it, this finger was wearing a ring. Some twisted person obviously wanted him to see it. He loosened the drawstring.

The finger slid onto his lap. It looked similar to the finger in the sink—except this one had a gold wedding band. And a familiar burn scar that ran from the nail to the second knuckle. His throat knotted. *Dad!*

Roaring filled his brain; dark blotches swooned before him. *How . . . ? What had happened to his parents?*

Somebody banged on the door. "Ship's security; open up."

It was Uncle James. He seemed taller than usual.

"Grab the little bastard!" Aunt Angelica shrilled in the hallway.

Austin tried squeezing past. Uncle James was a solid, beefy wall. "What did you do to them?" Austin screamed.

Now Aunt Angelica's contorted face stared directly into his, her eyes a malevolent green. How could she possibly be Dad's sister? "Loon's Landing is mine by rights," she said. "I'm oldest."

"I don't care about that friggin' cottage!" Riley's voice yelled. "Just let it go, will ya?"

"Don't you realize how much that place is worth? A couple of million, at least. You'd give *that* up?" Aunt Angelica's giddy laugh kindled a livid, answering hatred.

Austin slammed his head and shoulder into Uncle James' alcoholic gut. At the satisfying *oof!* he shoved through. In the hallway, passengers were staring and chattering in various languages.

He bolted for the stairwell and heard footsteps pounding behind him. Another erratic trail; foot catching on a post; tearing pain. . . . He kept going. Out swinging doors, wind cold in his face. Now, more sets of running footsteps. . . .

Where to? The stern, with its wicked, sucking water? No land in sight. Cell phone useless in his backpack. Out of breath, he paused by one of the boxy benches containing life jackets.

Then, suddenly . . . almost-silence. Except for his heart pounding in his ears. And a measured tread: Step, *scrunch*, step, *scrunch*. . . . "You are disturbed, Mr. Weekes. Let me help." A reptilian smile. Lethal snake eyes.

"*Forget it!*" Gasping, Austin focused on the lapel pin with its indecipherable name and paced sideways on his throbbing ankle. A hand extended in apparent goodwill—yet seen from the corner of his eye . . . the cold glint of a blade.

"Do it, steward!" Aunt Angelica screeched. "We'll take back your pay. Call Immigration, too."

He lunged, and bit down hard. Heard a crunch, hung on.

Somebody yelled. The steward was flung sideways, like a rag doll.

Astonishingly, Riley's bulky form sheltered him. "Here," he said. A life jacket slid over his head. Over Riley's head, too. "C'mon, we're outta here!"

"*No!* Those propellers . . . !" Austin glanced at the steward, who lay crumpled on the deck. Red gouges marked his hand in a bright, glistening crescent.

"*C'mon!*"

"James. . . . " Aunt Angelica was saccharine, wheedling. Austin edged backwards; her stance looked dangerous. An instant later, hands clawed at his face, his eyes. Hands with nine slashing fingernails. . . .

He blocked with his elbow and stomped on her foot.

In a burst of noise, his aunt was hauled off him. Austin stumbled and fell beside the steward. His hand landed on a cold blade; he grabbed the knife and tucked it safely in his pocket. Uncle James was slinking away—the coward.

A scream curdled his blood.

He lifted his head. Just in time to see a pair of feet—feet wearing gold sandals—disappear backwards, over the rail of the *Taku Spirit*.

Riley slumped against that same rail, panting. "Oh, *shit!*" he moaned.

# X X X X X

*Alison Lohans lives in Regina, Saskatchewan, and has published thirteen books. These include* Waiting for the Sun *(Red Deer Press, 2001),* Don't Think Twice, Laws of Emotion *and* Foghorn Passage. *Her books appear on Canadian Children's Book Centre "Our Choice" lists and have been shortlisted for awards, two winning readers' choice awards. Born in Reedley, California, Alison Lohans began inventing stories at the age of four and was first published when she was twelve. She does occasional teaching and research for the University of Regina, and in her free time plays cello, recorder, and cornet. Her vacation highlights include two Alaska cruises and a cruise of the Greek islands.*

# EVENING SHADE

## Gillian Chan

L ily sat on the churchyard wall. Through the thin cotton of her dress, she could feel the sharp edges of flint pressing into her thighs. She had worn her best dress, one she had made herself of white broderie anglaise. Now she was hoping that it had not been a mistake, that the moss on the wall would not stain it. She could just imagine the ribbing she'd get if that happened. "Wot you been up to, my girl, rolling around in the grass, eh?" Her dad would have a glint in his eye, but there'd be an edge to his voice all the same. Everyone said that Charlie Evans had a temper on him, but he rarely showed it with Lily. She sighed. That was going to change for certain, she just knew it. She didn't even want to think about that now; she had to sort out the business with John first. The fierce orange light of the setting sun caused her to squint as she stared down the lane, searching for him.

A figure, dark with a fiery nimbus, was approaching, but it looked too tall, a gangling shape, not at all like John's small, compact frame. Staring harder, Lily tried to make out if it was one of his friends; Stefan was that tall.

"John!" Her voice sounded high-pitched and shrill in her ears. Lily felt foolish. She knew it wasn't him. If it was Stefan, all she had done now was make herself look too eager, like she was the one in the wrong.

"Excuse me?" The voice was English, nothing like John's soft Canadian voice. The stranger stopped and turned so that he was facing Lily, who cursed under her breath when she felt a hot wash of color stain her cheeks.

"I'm sorry," she stuttered. "I thought you were someone else." Lily could see him clearly now that she was no longer staring into the sun. He was a boy of about sixteen, dressed in what looked like cricket whites, but he had odd shoes on, white leather with bright strips and swirls of color. *Clown shoes*, Lily thought to herself. She stifled the thought and the giggle that threatened to bubble from her throat when she looked at his face. It was blotchy, the eyes swollen and red rimmed. "Are you all right?" Lily asked, certain in her mind that the boy had been crying as he walked down the lane.

The boy hung his head and muttered something that Lily didn't catch and, as she continued to stare at him, he said more distinctly, "Yeah, I'm fine." His expression changed, his features hardening. "What's it to you anyway?"

Pursing her lips, Lily tossed her head, flicking her hair away from her face. "I was only asking. You looked a bit upset, that's all. No need for you to bite my head off."

Sighing, the boy leaned his back against the wall alongside where Lily sat. Glancing sideways up at her, he said, "I'm sorry. I didn't mean to be rude, and yeah, you're right, I am upset." He stared silently down at his feet.

Lily watched him, noticing the stillness of his body, the way his thick, dark hair sprang away from a double crown. It reminded her of her brother George; he had hair just like that. She fingered her own hair, wishing that hers was like that, instead of all curly. She took after her dad, even down to the same blonde color. John didn't seem to mind, though. He said it reminded him of the wheat that grew back home in Saskatchewan. She couldn't help smiling. It had taken her a while to get used to John's easy way with a compliment. There weren't that many at home, for sure. If her mum thought she was thinking too highly of herself, she was sure to bring Lily down. Mum would get a tight, pinched look on her face. "Don't you be putting on your parts, my girl," she'd say. "I'll not have people thinking that you've got ideas above your station."

Lily shivered, had the sudden sense that someone was watching her. The boy was staring at her, waiting for her to say or do something. "You're new here in Steeple Melling, aren't you? I haven't seen you before." Lily winced at how trite her words sounded. It was almost as bad as, "Do you come here often?" Lily grinned, because that *was* what John had said the first time they met. She hadn't laughed at him, so maybe this boy wouldn't laugh at her. Mind you, she was being a bit forward, talking to a stranger like this. He still hadn't said anything so she added, "I'm Lily Evans. I live in the cottages at the back of the churchyard."

Shaking himself like a dog coming out of water, the boy roused himself and laughed. "We have the same name, I'm Jeremy Evans—I suppose I am new. We only moved here in the spring. I grew up overseas. My dad's an engineer and he worked mainly in Canada and the States. He wanted to come back here, back to the place where he grew up. He's setting up a consulting business in Lowestoft." He looked appraisingly at Lily again. "Come to that, I haven't seen you before either, and I don't think we're long lost cousins or anything." He smiled suddenly.

Lily found herself smiling back at him. His smile changed his face completely. There was an openness that appealed to her, a feeling that this was his normal expression. It reminded her of John, who was always smiling. His friends called him Happy, after one of the dwarfs in *Snow White*. Her thoughts drifted again. She remembered going to see that film in Dereham; she and John had taken her little brother. John had held George on his lap after the wicked queen scared him. Lily smiled at the memory. John was good with George, never complaining about him tagging along. He would make a good father one day. A sigh penetrated her thoughts, and Lily realized that this Jeremy was looking up at her, impatient for her to acknowledge him. She took a deep breath. "Look, do you want to talk about what's upset you? You can tell me to mind my own business if you like. Margaret, she's my best friend, says I'm too nosy by half. But I think it's good to tell someone else your troubles, gets them into perspective. It did for me."

Lily squirmed, conscious that Jeremy was staring openly at her now.

"You don't look as if you have any troubles," he said. "When I was walking down the lane you looked so happy sitting there on the wall, swinging your legs, that it made me feel worse."

Lily couldn't help laughing then: he sounded so serious, like a little boy who wanted the world to be miserable because he was. "That's what you know. If you'd seen me yesterday, well, I was in a right pickle. I had a row with John, he's my boyfriend, right here where we are now." Lily felt the heat of tears pricking in her eyes. "He got some daft idea that I was interested in this other fellow, Len, and I'll be blowed if he'd listen when I tried to tell him that it was something and nothing. Stormed off back to the base he did, and I was just as bad." Lily felt the hot snail trail of a tear begin to edge down her cheek. "I shouted after him that I never wanted to see him again, ever!" She smiled down at Jeremy, a quick smile that left her face more solemn.

Jeremy's eyes widened and when he spoke his voice was shocked, "That's awful. I'd be really hurt if someone said that to me. Is John American? You said that he went back to the base."

Lily nodded. " Yes, he's up at the base, but he's Canadian, not American." Looking down at her lap, she spoke, her voice low and gentle, "I can tell you my parents were none too pleased when I started seeing him, but he's a nice bloke. They've got used to him now, and my kid brother, George, he thinks the sun shines out of John's backside." Lily giggled, covering her mouth with her hand like a naughty little girl. "My mum would be after me for that—she reckons that since I've been working, I've got really vulgar." Lily's expression changed, the smile vanished. "I reckon John being Canadian is half the reason we had that row."

Seeing Jeremy frown in puzzlement, Lily continued, "I grew up with Len, see. He's a couple of years older, but he's always been a bit sweet on me. Used to work with my dad on the grounds of the Manor. Well, he's always assumed that me and him had an understanding." Here, Lily bridled, her face flushing with annoyance. "Not with any encouragement from me though. He's in the service too, the RAF, and he came back on leave yesterday and came for his tea, just like he used to do." Lily laughed. "You should have seen his face when he found John was there; talk about being put out. Went all glum and silent, he did. It didn't help any when George kept telling him, 'John this' and 'John that,' how John had taken him and me to Norwich. Well, it made a big impression on George. Poor little beggar had never been to Norwich before." She looked at Jeremy, searching his face for signs that he understood. All she saw was puzzlement. "It got worse though," she continued. "I reckon that Len said something to John when they went out into the garden for a smoke, while I helped Mum do the crocks. Maybe a snide remark about Canadians getting the

English girls, just because they're different and a bit exotic round here." She sighed and looked down the lane. "I wonder where he can be, it's getting late."

Jeremy followed her glance but the lane was empty. The fierce orange of the sunset had faded now and a shadowy haze was settling on the lane between the hedgerows. Birds sang and, in the distance, an engine rumbled as it attempted to turn over. When he looked back, Lily's white dress seemed to glow in the dusk. "So, what makes you think this Len had a go?"

"Oh, no," Lily was flustered, "they didn't fight or anything. I didn't mean to give you that impression. It's just that when we went for a walk, after, John was quiet. We always stop here in the churchyard because it's just about the only private place we've got." She blushed slightly, her eyes glinting. "I'm sure those in here have seen a lot worse than me and my John having a bit of a kiss and cuddle." She lightly punched Jeremy's arm. "You must think I'm really wicked." Her smile vanished, as her eyes stared into the distance, remembering. "John did. He accused me of leading him on, not telling him that Len was my fiancé. My friend Margaret, her that I mentioned earlier, thinks Len told him that out of sheer spite. I went straight round hers after John left." Lily managed a tremulous smile. "Margaret got me sorted out; she's good at that. So, I sent a message to John to tell him to meet me here so I can explain, and," Lily paused, looking down at Jeremy, "to tell him my other news."

Lily looked so happy that, without thinking, Jeremy blurted out, "What other news?" Before Lily could answer, he rushed to say, "Not that you have to tell me of course—it's not any of my business."

Lily's blush deepened, the red of her cheeks seeming brighter in contrast to her white dress. "You might think it's a bit shocking, John and me not being wed, but, if you promise not to tell." Here, Lily stopped, not continuing until she saw

Jeremy nod. "Well, I went to the doctor in Dereham and I'm going to have a baby. I was going to tell John yesterday, but then we had that stupid row." Her smile returned and wavered as she spoke almost to herself, "John'll have calmed down by now. He flies off the handle right quick, but it don't last with him."

Jeremy smiled at Lily. "Why should I be shocked? People have babies all the time. I know tons of people who've had babies without being married."

Lily drew in her breath. "You must have been some right strange places then, before you came to Steeple Melling. Unless John and me can get a wedding sorted out soon, there's going to be a real to-do. I'm dreading telling me dad. I know his first thought will be to thump John." She tried a smile, but it didn't stick. "That's not fair though, is it? I'm as much to blame. If I can tell him without Mum being there, and sticking her twopen-north in, then maybe, I can keep him from flying off the handle."

Jeremy pulled a face. "What's it do with him. It's how you and John feel that counts. You seem pleased, and I'm sure John will be when you tell him." He patted Lily's arm, surprised how cool her skin felt.

She covered his hand with hers. "That's kind of you to say, but you don't know my family." She laughed, a brittle sound. "And you don't want to know them! But, you're right, John will be pleased. We've talked about getting married when things are more settled and we've even talked about kids. John's from a big family, and he thinks that you never feel lonely if you've got lots of brothers and sisters." Lily lifted her hand, waved it in front of her face where some midges were circling. "Listen to me going on. You've had my whole life story and you were going to tell me what upset you."

His mouth twisted into a wry smile, Jeremy hoisted himself up so that he sat on the wall alongside Lily. "I never actually said I was going to tell you, but, go on, I might as well. You can sort me out, like friend Margaret did for you." He laughed. "You're going to think it's all a bit trivial after what you've just told me. It's my girlfriend, Caroline."

"Nah." Lily shook her head so that her thick blonde curls bounced. "That's a bit of a posh name. She's not related to that snooty new family who's bought the Manor from the old Colonel, is she?" When Jeremy didn't answer, she added, "Go on then, what's happened?" Surreptitiously, Lily glanced at her watch and began to fiddle with the hem of her dress, pleating it between her fingers as she listened to Jeremy.

A thick lock of hair had fallen down over Jeremy's eyes and he swept it back impatiently. "Caroline goes to the private girls' high school in Norwich and one of her friends is having a party tomorrow night. I've not met any of her friends yet—I go to the comprehensive in Dereham and, anyway, we've only being going out since the summer holidays started. She asked me to go with her, but I've got to babysit my two little brothers. I promised my parents ages ago; they've got tickets for some play or other, and it's too late now to find anyone else." Jeremy hung his head.

"So what's the problem?" Lily stared hard at Jeremy. "You babysit and she goes to her friend's party. I don't see why you're in such a state about it."

"Ah," Jeremy gave her a rueful smile, "I think I behaved rather badly. I just assumed that she would stay with me. When she said she wanted to go to the party, I lost my temper and said some nasty things. I even accused her of being tired of me and wanting to pick up some wet private school boy. She said that if I was this immature, then she just might." Jeremy fell silent, studying his shoes. It was his turn to blush now.

Lily leaned over and patted his arm. "She don't mean it, not really, but you ought to sort things out with her. You don't want to let a silly quarrel like this hang over you. Just because you've got to stay in, doesn't mean she has to as well, especially when all her friends will be having a good time. She must think a lot of you if she wanted to show you off to them."

"Yeah, you're probably right." Jeremy's voice was ragged. "I've been a bit of an idiot. I don't know what's wrong. Everyone always says I'm quiet and shy and here I am losing my temper with Caroline over something really stupid, and then telling you, someone I've never met before all my troubles. You were right though, talking did help." He paused and struggled to make out Lily's face in the growing dusk. "What about your John though— shouldn't he be here soon? I don't want him coming along, seeing me and thinking you've got another boyfriend, apart from Len, that is." Jeremy's laugh, as he sprang down from the wall and landed on the tussock of grass and weed at its base, sounded fresh and young.

Lily's answer came from deep within the shadow cast by the church. Jeremy caught a glint of metal, a last bit of light catching her watch as she turned it to see the time. "He should have been here about half an hour ago. I know he got the message because George cycled out to the base for me this morning. John said he'd be here." Lily's voice was thickened by unshed tears. "It could be that his squadron's gone out on an op. I hope not though, I always worry when he's flying. He's a tail gunner in one of them Lancasters."

"Lancasters? I thought they flew F1-11's at the base?" Jeremy's voice cracked as he peered into the shadows. "You know, the ones they flew in the Gulf War."

Lily did not appear to have heard him. Her voice was quiet, almost as if she was talking to herself. "I hope they keep my John safe. He was saying that there were rumors about a big mission, some factory in Germany where they make ball bearings." Lily laughed, a high, defiant little laugh. "Ball bearings, my arse, what's the point of that? How's that going to slow that mad bugger Hitler down?" Her voice quavered, "Factories are always well defended though, lots of anti-aircraft guns and fighters. Last time they hit the Ruhr, they lost twenty planes. John showed me some bullets that came into his turret. Oh, I do hope he hurries up. . . ." Lily's voice trailed away into a papery whisper.

Jeremy stood still, suddenly cold despite the warm August evening. He moved slowly forward, one hand outstretched. All he felt was soft moss and hard flint as he ran his fingers over the top of the old wall.

## X X X X X

*Gillian Chan was born in England but has lived in Dundas, Ontario for fifteen years. Before becoming a full-time writer, she worked as bank clerk, bartender, letter sorter, and English teacher. If she wasn't a writer, she would like to have been a pastry chef. Her work is varied and includes short story collections, historical novels, and fantasy. Many of her books have been short listed for awards, including the Governor General's Award, the Red Maple Award, and the Diamond Willow Award. Her novel,* A Foreign Field, *won both the Nautilus Award and the White Pine Award.*

# THE HEALER

## Cheryl Rainfield

The stench of death fills my nostrils. It is sweet, cloying, overpowering. But it is not from the woman I am laying my hands on. The cancer that has been eating away at her liver is almost gone; I have been drawing the blackness up inside me, transforming it into light. I can feel her body working now to repair the damage. No, the smell of death is from someone else. Someone nearby.

Even as I send my mind out, searching the crowd, the pain begins, the way it always does when death is near. It starts at the soles of my feet and rises up my body, tearing at me, drawing the pain inwards, stretching upward until it fills my head, until my skull is throbbing with it. My skin tightens, my veins shrink, my mouth goes dry.

I have never told anyone how much it hurts me when death is close, never told anyone how I want to scream, how I want to do anything I can to end the pain. Never told anyone how it makes me want to wrench the dying back to the side of the living. I have never told anyone, because I'm afraid they'll think that's why I heal people. I am afraid they'll think I'm just selfish. I heal people because I have to. Because I can't bear to let anyone die—not like I did my sister. I heal them because I wouldn't like myself if I didn't try.

My hands are hot and trembling over the woman, the energy transferring from me to her. Death is piercing at my skull, but I can't let the woman go, not yet. I have to make sure the cancer doesn't return.

Waves of grief pass through me, but I shut them out and focus. I draw up the light from inside me and pour it into the woman's abdomen, giving one last surge. My skin feels like it is cracking all over. Death is near, very near, and it is in someone small.

I let the woman go and stagger backward.

"Thank you!" the woman cries, her cheeks rosy, her eyes bright with happiness and relief. Her face is so different now, the lines of pain smoothed out, the gaunt look gone. I feel myself grinning at her, warmth filling my whole body. There's nothing so good as the feeling of saving someone's life. It's brief moments like this that I feel glad for my talent. Blessed, even.

The pain grips me harder, and I close my eyes. I have to save this new life. I reach for the death, search for it. And just as I sense where it is, the life abruptly cuts off.

I open my eyes to see a squirrel fall from a branch above the crowd, its body stiff, too rigid for death that's just happened. People scream, pointing at the squirrel, at me, their shrieks hurting my ears. I know some will see this as a bad omen—another animal murdered in our town. And I know they will look to me as the cause.

The protesters on the edge of the group gain momentum, their voices ragged, their signs bobbing in angry fists.

"Devil's child!"

"She's interfering with God's will!"

"She's the harbinger of doom!"

I know they're only trying to control what they don't understand, trying to suppress their fear with superstitions—but it doesn't make me feel any better. And they're not the only ones who are afraid. Fear is something I've felt a lot lately.

The crowd is shouting and pushing forward, everyone wanting a turn. Only the two police officers are holding them back. People lose their sense of perspective when they are in pain. Pain or fear.

Mom comes to stand beside me, touching my shoulder. "Jamie? What is it?"

"It's the squirrel. It doesn't feel right. I have to go get it."

Mom's hand tightens on my shoulder. "Let someone bring it to you."

She scans the crowd for Terrence, signals to him, but he is not watching her. He is watching the crowd, a grim look on his face.

My brother was the first person besides me who realized what I could do. When I was two and he was five, Terrence stomped on a grasshopper and crushed it flat, right in front of me. I shrieked when the life snuffed out of it, shrieked with the pain of death still vibrating in my bones. When my head had cleared, I'd picked the grasshopper up, cradled it in both my hands, and told it to come alive—and it did. The smushed-out guts drew back into the grasshopper, the flattened parts of it bulged, and the body twitched. It came alive, scraped its legs together, and jumped off my hand.

Terrence had stared at me, eyes wide, and then he'd backed away from me, like he was afraid of me. I tried to touch him, but his eyes were so full of fear, I could feel it right in the center of my heart. I stood and watched him walk away, and that pretty much sums up our relationship. He still does everything he can to avoid me, and I just let him. You can't force anyone to like you.

I sometimes wonder if things would have been different between me and Terrence, between me and my whole family, if Mom and Dad hadn't found out. But they did.

I didn't understand my talent when I was little. Bringing someone back to life was just a reflex, an instinctive reaction. But the complexity of healing a person takes more than instinct. It takes practice and knowledge.

My sister got cancer when I was six, and Mom was desperate for me to cure her. "Focus," she'd say. "Focus, Jamie. You can do it." We'd sit there for hours, Mom and Cindy and me, as I tried to draw out the cancer. Mom wouldn't let anyone interrupt; she knew I needed to concentrate. I'd see Terrence standing in the doorway, sometimes, looking awkward and lonely, but Mom never invited him in, and I didn't care. I was too involved in what I was doing. Too sure that I was saving Cindy.

Cindy would get better, then worse, then better again. But finally she seemed to make a full recovery, and I, along with everyone else, thought that I'd cured her. But I didn't know that disease can sit inside us, undetectable—and that to heal a fatally ill person, to really heal them, I have to heal past when I think I'm done. I have to reach for the remnants of disease that even I can't detect, and draw them all out.

Cindy died when she was away at camp. By the time I got there, too much time had passed for me to bring her back. I think Mom blamed me. I know I do. I should have known better, should have been able to feel it. I still play that night over and over in my mind, wishing I'd been able to bring her back. But even in my dreams, I never do.

Sometimes I wish I could just end it all now, never have to see another desperate face again. Never have to fall into bed at night, bones aching. But I think of Cindy's eyes, of how they pleaded with me to heal her, and I keep going. I always keep going.

Mom shouts at Terrence again, and he nods, then starts shoving his way through the crowd. He's built like an ape on steroids, so it's easy for him. Everyone gets out of his way. He pushes his way back to me, the dead squirrel tiny in his huge hands. He looks like he wants to say something, but I don't have time to try to draw it out of him. I can feel the energy gushing out of the squirrel, much faster than normal.

I lay my hands on its sides and reach inside, pour the energy of life into it. It stirs, sits up, shakes its head, then leaps from my hand to the porch railing, and up into the trees. The crowd gasps, flashbulbs burst in my eyes. I know they are seeing my gray skin, my bloodshot eyes and trembling hands, my mouth drawn back tight over my teeth. I know they are seeing the way I am swaying, the way I am leaning on Mom for support. I know because I've seen photos of me after I've brought someone back from the dead. It drains me to my core, but I still have to do it.

"She's evil. Get away from her before she poisons you!" a protester yells, his skin stretched tight over his bones, his eyes gleaming, his face distorted with rage. He hardly looks human.

Mom's waving to the officers to push the crowd back, the crowd that takes up our whole front yard and spills out over the street and down the block. "That's all for today, folks. Jamie's tired."

People groan, they curse and boo me, but they start to depart.

Mom drags me upright, a worried look on her face. "You should tell me when you're tired. You push yourself too hard!"

"But I can do more," I say. "I know I can."

"You don't always have to do more. What you do is a gift," Mom says. "Why do you push yourself so hard?" But she already knows the answer. She looks away before I do.

There's something in the way Terrence is watching the crowd that makes me think he enjoys seeing their disappointment.

I bite my lip. What he really enjoys is seeing *me* disappoint them. The wonder girl isn't such a wonder. What he doesn't get is that I already know that. I knew that the first time I failed to save someone. Failed to save Cindy. And yet all the attention gets showered on me. It must be hard to live in the same house as me. People always reaching out to touch me, to photograph me, not even seeing him for the handsome jock he is. In any other family, he'd be the star.

I know he's jealous of me, and that just twists my stomach, because I'm jealous of him—of his easy relationship with Dad, the way he can get Dad to talk to him, and the way he can laugh with Mom, and let her nag at him, give him advice. They never treat me like that. Not in all the years since they found out, have they treated me like that. I feel more like a guest in my own house than their flesh and blood.

A squirrel chatters from the roof, and I wonder if it's the same one I saved. I take a deep, shuddering breath. The way the squirrel died wasn't natural. It felt like someone was drawing the life out of it—the way I push life back in. I stare up at the tree. There is someone out there with a power like mine.

I have always sensed it was there inside me—the ability to take life energy away, as well as to give it, but I have never let myself go near that ability. Never even been tempted by it. But someone else has.

I lick my dry lips. I'm terrified that might be true, and yet at the same time, I almost want it to be. I've felt alone for so long. Felt different, other. I know that's how people see me; some look at me like I'm a freak, others look at me like I'm a god. Most only look at me for what they can get from me. No one ever looks at me for me.

I know Mom tries; Dad tries, too. But even they have trouble. Mom glorifies my abilities, Dad sometimes seems afraid of me. And if even they fail to see me as their daughter, as just a regular fifteen-year-old girl with hopes and dreams and insecurities, how can I expect anyone else to?

The squirrel angrily chatters as Mom leads me into the house, and I clap my hand over my mouth. How could I not have seen it? The squirrel's death ties in with all the other animals that have been murdered around town this week. All those pets—cats and dogs and even a ferret—and the sparrows and squirrels, too—they were all stiff with death when they were found, not a scratch or broken bone among them, just emaciated statues, like the life had been sucked out of them.

And I didn't feel any of them die. Not one of them, even though some only died a few blocks away. I feel the weight of their deaths like their bodies piled on my back. Because I am sure, now, that their deaths had something to do with me. Someone doesn't like what I do. Someone doesn't like the healing I bring. And they're trying to get me to stop.

I stagger to the table, leaning heavily on Mom. Dad's already home; he came in the back way, avoiding the crowd. Avoiding me. Terrence barrels in, the door slamming shut after him, and he starts gulping down the chili Dad made, almost before he's seated.

I stuff a forkful in my mouth, but I can't taste it. All those deaths are all my fault. I move the food around my plate and try to smile, try not to worry my parents further. Mom's hardly spoken since she sat down at the table. Dad's quiet, too, avoiding my gaze. He knows something's happened, but he doesn't want to know what. I can sense it in him, the fear of knowing, the not wanting to talk, in the way his jaw is clenched, the way he holds himself so tight.

Terrence is chewing louder than normal, every click of his jaw like a hand slapping a fist. I know he hates the time Mom spends on the porch with me, know he hates being pressured into appearing, into helping the two of us keep some order.

He'd rather be out with his buddies, laughing and drinking and talking football. But he does it for Mom. I think he does it to make her love him. What he doesn't know is that she loves him already. She probably loves him more than me.

I ask Terrence about his day, but he doesn't respond, doesn't even acknowledge my questions until Mom asks them as if they're her own. I know he talks about me with his friends, laughs at me behind my back. Jealousy and fear—they're all twisted inside him. Sometimes I think I should just give up healing, that maybe it would help Terrence, help my whole family, but I know I could never do that. I could never let people die. And, if I'm honest with myself, I could never give up the rush I get, the feeling of being able to do something so powerful and right. Something that even doctors can't do.

Terrence looks at me across the table, and it's like he can see that in my eyes. He rakes his chair back. "I'm going out."

Mom puts down her fork. "Where are you going? Don't you have homework?"

"What do you care?" Terrence stalks towards the door, and for a moment, we are all still.

"Get your butt back here!" Dad yells, half rising, but Terrence keeps going. Dad's jaw clenches, the darkness in him rising, and the worry rises in Mom like a storm.

I put my napkin down. "I'm going out after him."

"All right, Jamie," Mom says, her eyes anxious. "But don't be too long. You still have homework to do."

I can feel Dad gearing up to object, and I get out of there fast.

The sun is already setting, turning the sky a pink orange, leeching out the blue above. The trees cast shadows over my skin, and I shiver, wondering what I'm doing going after Terrence when I'm so tired, when I know he'll never listen to me.

I look down the street, first left, then right, but I don't see him, don't even see his red shirt. He's fast on his feet when he wants to be, and I am like an old woman tottering along, my joints aching, my legs unsteady in the odd way they've been all week. He could be anywhere.

I lean up against the oak tree on our lawn, wrap my arms around it, and I feel the energy rushing back into me. It's almost as if trees heal me with their wisdom, the sap running through them like energy.

I feel my body relax, my breathing deepen, before someone's anger pierces my skull. It has to be Terrence. I push myself away from the tree, and start down the street.

I haven't gone thirty steps before I smell it—the stench of death, thick and sweet, rising in my nostrils. I feel it, too, in the tightening of my veins, in the dryness of my mouth. Someone or something is dying.

I let myself give in to the pain until I am shaking with it, until I am almost crying out. And then I am running toward it, feet pounding against the pavement, eyes half shut against the tears. I stumble, pavement hitting my knees, splitting through my jeans, the pain so great I can't see.

I reach forward blindly, and touch the warm, furry body of a puppy, lying still. It's stiff, not even its paws twitching, and its energy is fading quickly.

The murderer did this—the murderer with my power. My stomach turns, but I can't let myself think about that now. I rest my hands on the small body, drawing up energy from inside me, funneling it into the puppy's lungs and heart and veins, until I can feel its heart pumping beneath me, can feel its body wiggle, trying to get up.

I let go, the pain receding from my mind. The puppy licks my face, whimpering happily, and I know it knows, the way animals do, that I have brought it back to life. It licks me harder with its rough, warm tongue, licks my chin and mouth and nose. I laugh, my vision clearing, and I can see the brown puppy now, can see its tail, its whole body wagging, and I know it is thanking me in the way it can.

"You're welcome, little one. You're very welcome."

I pat its rump and stand. "You coming with me?" I start forward, thinking the puppy will follow, but it whines and hangs back.

I crouch down, wondering if I've missed something, but I don't sense pain anywhere in the puppy, only fear.

And that is when I notice it again—the gradual tightening of my skull, the pain crawling over my skin, the sickly sweetness filling the air.

It's happening again.

My legs buckle. I run towards the pain, and it sucks me in, washing over me, eating at my skin like fire. It's not just one life this time. It's two. Maybe three.

My breath is harsh in my throat. I can't see beyond the spots in my eyes, but still I run. And I know by the pain when I am there. I kneel down.

There are three cats, a mother and her kittens, lying still. Though they are warm, their energy has almost faded. I lay one hand on the mother, one hand on the kittens, and pull from my center, pull the way I never have before for the energy that I know is there, the energy that has to be there.

The pain does not fade, even after they are mewing and moving beneath my hands. If anything, it is worse, slicing through my skull a blade, and tugging at my chest, my heart, making it hard to breathe. I am almost choking on the smell, on the sweetness that is pushing into my face, smothering the air.

But the cats are alive and healthy. I let them go, and they run away, not staying like animals usually do.

The pain tightens my skin, draws me on. I stagger forward, knowing I am leading myself into a trap, but I can't turn my back on another life.

This is insane. I know it is, and I know, too, that I'm the only one who can fight this killer. But I don't know how to stop it all, don't know how to help except by bringing life where there is death—and I can't do that much longer.

I am crying, now, crying so hard I can hardly breathe, the sweetness like bile in my throat, and at first I don't hear his voice.

"Jamie," he says. He says it again.

Sound moves in and out of my ears in waves. I stagger, stop. "Terrence, thank God!" The pain is so bad I can hardly think. "There's someone out here murdering animals. You've got to help me!"

"I am helping you." His voice is louder than normal. Larger. Almost swollen with sound.

I blink my eyes, try to see past the tears, past the spots of light and dark. The pain of death is beneath my skin, now, pushing up through my flesh. It is so strong I almost want to claw at my body to get rid of it.

I blink again, and there is Terrence, his chest puffed out, his face almost glowing, and a thin smile on his face. I draw in a ragged breath. The pain, the feeling of death, is coming from him. That feeling I had while working with the crowd, that feeling I've had for weeks—an undercurrent of death reaching into my skull, drawing away my energy, drawing me towards death—it's all coming from Terrence.

"I'm helping you be normal." Terrence's lips brush against my ear. "For once in your life, I'm helping you fail. Maybe then you'll know what it's like not to be perfect."

His words echo in my mind, but they don't make sense. I'm not perfect. I never have been. I failed to save my own sister. And there's so many people I don't save—people all over the world.

I don't even have any friends. Terrence is Mr. Popularity; I'm the strange kid all the others are afraid of. Even Dad isn't comfortable with me; he never has been. It's Terrence he likes. It's Terrence he tries to talk to.

"I'm not perfect."

Terrence laughs, his breath hot on my cheek. "Everybody thinks you are. You're the special one, the media darling. The one people line up for weeks to see. It makes me sick! But guess what—you're not the only one who's special. I can do something nobody else can do, not even you. I can manipulate dormant genes, bring disease out of hiding. I can even kill a person if I focus on them long enough—and I don't even have to touch them to do it. I'm stronger than you, Jamie. More powerful. How does it feel to know that?"

I am gasping, now, wanting to tear the words out of my skull, but I am too weak to back away.

Terrence wraps his fingers around my wrist, and I feel my veins begin to flatten, can feel my body start to shut down.

"But it doesn't really matter, does it?" Terrence says. "No one will ever like me for that. You're the one who saves people. You're the one everyone thinks is a god. How can I compete with that?"

My head feels like it is cracking open, but I have to fight to live. I have to fight for both of us.

I reach inside, but the energy is so faint I almost can't find it. I close my eyes against the pain, and think of the smile on the woman's face today, think of the love in Mom's voice. The energy grows stronger.

"You don't have to compete," I say. "A lot of people look up to you. You make people comfortable, Terrence, when you're not angry. You make people feel good."

Terrence laughs again, his voice rough with emotion, but the pain slackens a little.

I pull the energy up through my veins, and let it flow through me. But as fast as I pull it up, I can feel Terrence siphoning it off. I am gagging on the sweetness of death, choking on it. Choking on my own smell. Death is near, and I can't hold it back.

I am on my knees, the life draining from me fast. There is pain in every cell of my body. I know I can slow this, maybe even halt this, if I fight his way, if draw the life energy from him into myself, and I want to, I desperately want to. I'm not ready to die. But still I hesitate. I'm not sure if I can kill my brother to save myself. Yet I must. If I let him kill me, he will go on to kill others. No one will suspect what he can do. And no one will be able to stop him.

I draw breath into my tight lungs, breath that hurts, and then I grip onto Terrence with one hand, and reach inside him with my mind.

The stench of death is so strong that I almost pull out, but I cannot. I cannot let him go. I start to draw on his life force, start to pull it towards me, but it feels wrong. And even as I try to draw it out, I feel him sucking up mine, faster than I can focus. He is so much more skilled at this than me. He has been practicing.

I try to move, to back away, and the sidewalk tilts sickeningly, Terrence's laugh echoing in my ears. I think I'm going to vomit.

I draw on the last of the energy faltering inside me—and then I change its flow. I stop pulling at his energy, and draw instead on his darkness, his longing for death. I draw it out as hard as I can, as if it is an illness, and I let the energy transform it. And as I do, I sense the light in his heart, the light he's kept hidden, even from himself. I focus on that light, pour myself into it, and I feel it swell, growing faster than I'd thought it could.

I send him more energy, and then he is trying to pull away from me, not me from him, but I don't let him; I can't. There is still darkness inside him, and I cannot loosen my grip. It is like a death grip, as if all life depends on it, and in that moment, it feels like it does.

My thoughts are slowing down, and I ache with exhaustion, but still I send the healing through his body, until that is all I feel. And then I let him go, and collapse against the sidewalk, my heart beating erratically.

The pain is lifting from me, my energy sluggishly returning. And with it comes the awareness of how to shield. I draw up light within myself, draw it on me like armor, and there is no more pain, just a weariness that makes me want to lie here forever.

"Jamie," Terrence says, his voice a croak.

I rest my head against the pavement, and try to push his hands away.

"Jamie," he says, salt tears falling on my cheek. His energy flows into me, and I open my eyes to see him crying.

He gathers me into his strong arms, and I feel my heart beat stronger, my thoughts quicken.

"I'm sorry, so sorry," he says. "I didn't know what I was doing. I wanted to be like you, to get Mom's attention like you did, to be the one to save Cindy. I tried, I swear I did, but all I could do was find death." His voice falters. "The way it found Cindy."

"It wasn't your fault Cindy died," I say. "We both did the best we could. We were just kids, Terrence. Just kids."

The energy is pushing into me fast, swelling my veins, letting me breathe again. The pain is fading, and I feel full of happiness, a bittersweet happiness I have never known, and it's coming from Terrence. I know he's giving me a chance to live—the way I've given that to so many people.

The old layer of guilt dissolves inside me, and I sit up. My life is important, too. I know Cindy would think that. I will keep healing people; life is too important to toss away. But I'm going to take more time to enjoy things. Going to spend more time on me—and more time with my family. Because even if nobody else ever sees me, I can see myself. And it's not so bad, what I see.

I can feel Mom's worry, stretching out the blocks towards us, can feel her wondering where we are, and I wonder what she'll think when she sees us together. I smile widely. We have found each other, Terrence and I. We have become true family.

Terrence is crying still. "Forgive me," he says, over and over. "Forgive me."

"Of course I forgive you," I say. I reach for his hand, press it against my cheek. "Things will be all right, now. You'll see."

And I know that they will be.

# X X X X X

*Cheryl Rainfield has written ever since she could pick up a pen and form words. Cheryl has been an avid reader for as long as she can remember, and a keen observer of the people around her. Her writing often draws on her experience of child abuse and healing. Cheryl is a member of CANSCAIP (Canadian Society of Children's Authors, Illustrators, and Performers) and SCBWI (Society of Children's Book Writers and Illustrators). She lives in Toronto with her partner, her dog, and her two cats.*